Big Bang!

Auntie raised her mike to advise the crowd to stay for the big finale. "You ain't seen nothin' folks. Stick around." Then she waved Mr. Eng over. It was time for the big firecracker finale.

Lifting up her mike again, Auntie caught Mr. Eng's shoulder and pulled him in closer. "Mr. Eng, the Fishers of the Wok Inn are proud to present you with this ball of money, totaling two thousand dollars."

"Thank you," Mr. Eng said loudly. "This will be a double feast—a lunch for me and a generous donation for the foundation."

As Auntie stepped back, she motioned to the ever-present Bernie. "Get ready."

Bernie took out a book of matches and got ready to strike one. "Right, Miss T."

I glanced up nervously at the long, dangling fire-cracker strings and took a couple of long side steps away from them.

And then the whole world seemed to explode.

ALSO BY LAURENCE YEP

Sweetwater

Dragonwings
A 1976 Newbery Honor Book

Child of the Owl

The Serpent's Children

Mountain Light

The Rainbow People

Tongues of Jade

Dragon's Gate
A 1994 Newbery Honor Book

Thief of Hearts

The Dragon Prince

The Imp That Ate My Homework

CHINATOWN MYSTERIES

The Case of the Goblin Pearls
Chinatown Mystery #1

The Case of the Firecrackers
Chinatown Mystery #3

DRAGON OF THE LOST SEA FANTASIES

Dragon of the Lost Sea

Dragon Steel

Dragon Cauldron

Dragon War

EDITED BY LAURENCE YEP

American Dragons
Twenty-Five Asian American Voices

LAURENCE YEP

The Case of the
LION
DANCE

CHINATOWN

Mystery
#2

■ HarperTrophy®
A Division of HarperCollinsPublishers

The Case of the Lion Dance
Copyright © 1998 by Laurence Yep
All rights reserved. No part of this book may be used or reproduced in any manner
whatsoever without written permission except in the case of brief
quotations embodied in critical articles and reviews.
Printed in the United States of America. For information address
HarperCollins Children's Books, a division of HarperCollins Publishers,
10 East 53rd Street, New York, NY 10022.

Library of Congress Cataloging-in-Publication Data
Yep, Laurence.
    The case of the lion dance / Laurence Yep.
        p.   cm. — (Chinatown mystery ; #2)
    Summary: When $2000 is stolen during the opening of a restaurant, Lily and her aunt,
a Chinese American movie actress, search for the thief throughout San Francisco's
Chinatown.
    ISBN 0-06-024447-X.   ISBN 0-06-024448-8 (lib. bdg.)
    ISBN 0-06-440553-2 (pbk.)
    [1. Mystery and detective stories.   2. Chinese Americans—Fiction.   3. Chinatown
(San Francisco, Calif.)—Fiction.]   I. Title.   II. Series: Yep, Laurence.   Chinatown ; 2.
PZ7.Y44Cau   1998   97-49664
[Fic]—dc21   CIP
                                                                                                                 AC

Typography by Al Cetta
❖
First Harper Trophy edition, 1999

Visit us on the World Wide Web!
http://www.harperchildrens.com

TO SUSAN MEYERS AND HER INTREPID P. J. CLOVER

CHAPTER ONE

*B*um-ba-ba-bum. Bum-ba-ba-bum.

With legs spread, the drummer struck the surface of the heavy, red cylindrical drum. His muscles stood out in cords on his back. His sticks became a blur as the sound thundered down the street through the tall canyon formed by the skyscrapers of the financial district and the smaller valleys created by the Chinatown buildings.

I felt my pulse match the beat—as if the drummer controlled my heart. Next to him, his rival began to strike his own drum in counterpoint.

Before the new Chinese restaurant stood a forest of green shrubbery rising from dozens of pots wrapped in red foil. Red ribbons dangled from the sides. The Chinese characters on them were wishes for good luck and prosperity on the restaurant's opening. More ribbons with good wishes had been taped to the insides of the windows. They were written in what Auntie assured me was elegant Chinese calligraphy.

Across the doorway stretched an even longer red

ribbon, which the deputy mayor was to cut with a pair of huge scissors. Inside there were tablecloths, and roses in vases, and napkins folded up like birds.

The Wok Inn was to feature a trendy menu mixing Chinese and French cooking. The Chinese dumplings were stuffed with goose pâté rather than ground pork. The cabbage à la Bretonne used Chinese cabbage. Auntie had put on ten pounds sampling the dishes and helping to set the menu.

Auntie had scheduled the opening at lunchtime, so a crowd of business types in suits and ties and bows was gathering. Down Columbus were even more flooding out of the skyscrapers in search of a meal and heading toward us, drawn by the booming drums. Tourists here for Easter vacation and Chinese were coming from Chinatown.

I was just making a last-minute check before the beginning of the lion dance contest. Morgan and Ann Fisher had once run the Ciao Chow, which was of one of the fanciest and most popular restaurants in San Francisco. Now they were trying to start a new one, the Wok Inn. And they had asked my great-aunt, Auntie Tiger Lil, to help publicize it. She'd come up with the idea of having a lion dance contest between two martial arts schools to draw in a crowd. Naturally enough, one of the schools had been Barry Fisher's. He was Morgan and Ann's son. He and Akeem, another boy I knew, were getting ready for the contest.

Suddenly I heard a boy shout, *"You'll never win!"* in Chinese. And he added a string of insults.

I turned to see a boy about my age, twelve. His head

was completely shaved. Like my friends Akeem and Barry, he wore a T-shirt and loose black pants tucked into white socks, so I assumed he was also involved in the martial arts but was one of their rivals in the coming contest.

Barry held up his hands, trying to calm the boy down while Akeem said, "Speak English, Kong."

Kong looked around and focused on me. "*Look at these dogs,*" he announced loudly for the spectators. "*They can't even speak Chinese, and yet they ape us.*"

I made my way through the growing crowd to head off a fight. "*What trouble?*" I asked in my broken Chinese.

Kong seemed puzzled. Thinking he had not heard me, I yelled the same thing. Instantly his expression changed to contempt, making me wonder if I had used the wrong words or flubbed the tones. I understood Chinese better than I spoke it.

"*The only thing worse than them*"—he jerked a thumb at Barry and Akeem—"*is a Chinese who can't speak Chinese.*" He sneered.

"*I try learn,*" I said feebly.

"*You're nothing but empty bamboo,*" Kong said. "*Yellow on the outside, hollow on the inside.*"

At that moment, though, Barry and Akeem's teacher, Professor Sheng, strolled over. He was a small, stocky man who wore loose black pants and a short black cotton jacket with red piping.

"*Be quiet,*" he ordered. "*Treat even your rivals with respect.*"

Kong stared insolently at Professor Sheng. "*Why did

you have to choose him?" He pointed at Barry. *"It's an insult to have to compete with a half-breed!"*

Professor Sheng sucked in his breath, squaring his shoulders and holding his head erect. *"Apologize."*

Barry and Akeem had not understood one word of this whole exchange, but Barry seemed to understand the tone, at least. He whispered into Akeem's ear and then went into a crouch, as if he were riding a horse.

"If you've got a problem with Barry," Akeem said, "he's willing to settle it."

Professor Sheng turned sternly to Barry and Akeem. "Learn to curb your anger." He spoke English with a slight British accent.

While he thought Barry was distracted, Kong suddenly kicked out his leg. Barry must have seen the movement from the corner of his eye; he managed to catch Kong's foot. For a moment Kong hopped up and down on his other foot. Then Barry gave a shove, and Kong fell on his backside.

Kong jumped to his feet immediately. "I kill you!" he screamed in English.

Barry went into his stance again. "Try it."

There might have been a battle right there on the sidewalk, but Professor Sheng stepped between them. *"You are a disgrace,"* he said to Kong.

At that moment a tall, skinny man in his seventies came over. He had the rigid posture of a career soldier. He had on a satin robe and black coat, and on his head was a black cap. He looked like one of the photos of Chinese mandarins I'd seen in a book.

4

As soon as Kong saw him, he came to stiff attention.

"Kong, get ready for the contest," the man said. I assumed the man was Kong's teacher, Master Wang, from Chinatown.

Professor Sheng fought to control his temper. *"Your student should apologize to mine."*

Master Wang gazed scornfully at Professor Sheng. *"For what? You've bastardized our art and prostituted our discipline."*

Professor Sheng began to crouch as Kong had done. *"I've shared our teachings with all people."*

Master Wang was smiling as he took up the same stance. *"They don't belong to mongrels."*

Because of Kong's reaction to my Chinese, I used English. "Please—this is supposed to be a friendly contest."

Professor Sheng glanced at me and then straightened slowly. "Lily is right," he said. "This is supposed to be a happy occasion. We're opening a wonderful new restaurant."

Master Wang's lip curled up on one side. "I knew you'd find an excuse to back out of a fight." He nodded to Kong. *"Come. They're all cowards. There's no honor fighting with them."*

With a contemptuous toss of his head, Kong followed his teacher.

"What was that all about?" Akeem asked in frustration. He and Barry were my schoolmates at Morris Sachs Middle School.

"I don't approve of Master Wang's methods," Professor

Sheng explained in English, "and apparently he doesn't approve of mine."

I looked over toward Master Wang's students. They were busy helping Kong into his lion costume. They were all Asian. In contrast to Master Wang, whose school was in Chinatown, Professor Sheng had a studio out in the Richmond district toward the ocean, so his students were Afro-Americans, Hispanics and whites as well as Asians.

"Are all Master Wang's students Asian?" I asked.

Professor Sheng sighed. "In fact, Master Wang restricts his teachings even among Asians. He won't have Koreans and Japanese, let alone non-Asians."

I was shocked. "But that's—"

"Prejudice?" The professor raised an eyebrow. "Prejudice can work two ways. Master Wang thinks Chinese secrets belong only to Chinese."

Akeem grinned and slapped Barry on the back. "So it will hurt even worse to lose to us."

Barry's cheeks turned red. He was unaccustomed to so much attention. In fact, he was so shy that he almost never spoke out loud. He whispered now into Akeem's ear.

"Barry wants to know what Kong was saying," Akeem said to me.

"Nothing you should pay attention to," Professor Sheng said calmly.

Barry said something to Akeem again.

"I can't say that," Akeem said, glancing at their teacher.

"What is it?" Professor Sheng asked kindly.

Akeem swallowed. "Barry hopes you didn't choose him just because his parents own the new restaurant."

The Professor put his hand on Barry's shoulder. "I chose you because you are the best. You'll make our school proud."

I looked over to the other side. Kong was doing some kind of exercise, his arms and legs whipping violently through the air. "Do you think he'll try to hurt Barry?" I asked.

"Let him try," Akeem said. "Barry will hand his teeth back to him."

"A true warrior doesn't have to fight," Professor Sheng said, and he pointed to the costume's elaborate lion's head.

I think a real lion might have been scared by it. The head was squat and round. It looked like a red-and-yellow pumpkin with red-and-silver eyeballs that bounced and jiggled. There were big bushy white eyebrows, and the skin was painted red and gold. The mouth was hinged, with the lower jaw formed by a flat flap. The lion's body was formed by a red cape with golden curls painted in big, bold curves.

"Just prove me right in my choice. Stop thinking about Kong, and focus on the contest."

With Akeem on one side and the professor on the other, Barry went to rejoin his school.

I looked at Master Wang and his students. They all looked stuck-up. I suppose they considered themselves the only true Chinese in the group. Kong's contempt stung me. Even though I had Chinese parents, he felt I didn't count because I didn't speak the language well.

I found myself hoping that the bigots would lose; but if they did, there was probably going to be lots of trouble. I'd better warn Auntie.

CHAPTER TWO

I found Auntie holding a ladder in front of the restaurant, supervising a plump woman in a green waitress uniform as she hung up the last string of firecrackers. The strings were about six feet long and dangled like giant red millipedes.

The woman was one of those Chinatown waitresses who all seemed to be cast from the same mold—plump builds and bowl-shaped hairdos that looked like they had been sprayed to last till doomsday. They were indestructible, outlasting food fads, restaurants and owners.

"That's good, Bernie," Auntie told the woman.

"I never had a head for heights, Miss T," Bernie said as she climbed down from a sign so new that the paint still looked wet. It was suspended by wires some twenty feet overhead.

"I'd have gone up myself, but it's kind of hard to climb in this dress," Auntie said. Somehow she had squeezed into a red silk dress with gold patterns and piping, but there were bulges where Auntie had put on weight.

"Auntie?" I called.

Auntie ignored me.

When Bernie had set foot on the sidewalk again, she asked solicitously, "Can I get you something cold to drink?"

Auntie shook her head. "I got to keep the pipes loose and warm for show time."

Bernie looked stricken. "I didn't think. I'm sorry."

Auntie patted her shoulder. "You couldn't have known."

Bernie rapped her own knuckles against her forehead. "Sometimes I think I'm so stupid."

Auntie tried to comfort her. "We couldn't have opened this place without you, Bernie. You're the glue holding everything together."

"That's nice of you to say," Bernie said—though she didn't look as if she believed Auntie. "But can't I get you anything?"

"Well, I guess my throat may be getting a little tight. Got any hot tea?" Auntie asked.

"Have we got tea!" Bernie bragged. "We've got more tea than China." She was so plump that she had trouble bending over to duck under the ribbon across the doorway.

As she hustled inside, Auntie looked at the growing mob. By now the onlookers had blocked the sidewalk and were even spilling out into the street.

"Not a bad crowd, hey, kiddo?" Auntie asked, catching sight of me. "I'm good at this. Maybe I should concentrate just on publicity."

I was shocked. "Give up your movie career?" For

decades, Auntie had been Ms. Show Biz.

Auntie waved a hand at the jammed sidewalk. "I've got a knack for publicity. I've even had an offer from a big downtown firm, but it would mean working full-time."

I was sorry I couldn't let Auntie enjoy her moment. "Auntie, did you know there was bad blood between Master Wang and Professor Sheng?"

When Auntie looked at me blankly, I thought she hadn't heard me over the drums, so I repeated myself in a shout.

Suddenly Auntie held up her index finger. "Wait a mo'." Putting a hand to the side of her head, she removed something from her ear. "When I knew I was going to be around big drums, I got these earplugs out again. When I went to Italy to film my first spaghetti western, I kept flinching every time a gun went off. So Clint told me to try these. I have to read lips to understand what people are saying."

When I repeated my question a third time, she rolled her eyes. "I was just trying to get the best two schools. I didn't think they'd act like teamsters and electricians on a movie. I'll keep an eye on them." Nothing fazed Auntie, from runaway elephants in a Tarzan movie to Mongol warriors.

"When you said Clint, you didn't mean *the* Clint Eastwood, did you?" I asked.

Auntie knew a lot of famous people, some of whom were still famous. "I knew him when he used to do bit parts. When I heard he had gone to Italy, I thought

I'd try my luck there too. We were in a little spaghetti western called *Stagecoach from Hell*." She winced. "The stagecoach had no springs, and the saddle horses were worse. I had to sleep on my stomach for months afterward. I won't miss that part of show biz."

Bernie reappeared, fussy as a little old hen. "Miss T, the tea's brewing. Do you want me to turn on the fan now?" she asked from behind the ribbon in the doorway.

Auntie snapped her fingers. "Thanks for reminding me, Bernie. Yes, I'd say it's time."

Bernie dipped her head, smiling her ever-present smile. "You got it, Miss T." And she disappeared inside again.

Auntie sighed as she watched her leave. "What a treasure she is. But if I hear her talk one more time about her varicose vein operation, I'll scream."

I looked at the sky. It was clear but cold. "Isn't it a little cool for fans?" I asked, puzzled.

"They're to blow the kitchen aromas outside." Auntie winked. "There's more than one way to skin a tourist." There were a lot of visitors during Easter vacation.

A breeze came from inside the restaurant, wafting out heavenly aromas.

Auntie sniffed the air. "I love this gig."

Her dress looked a little strained over her belly. "You have gained a little weight, haven't you, Auntie?" I asked.

Auntie glanced longingly toward the restaurant's kitchen. More than anyone else, she knew what delights Ann had been concocting for the opening. "Just a little," she said defensively.

I pinched her love handles. "When you weighed

yourself this morning, you said you thought a horse had gotten on the scales with you."

She shrugged. "Who cares, kiddo? If I take that job, I can buy a new wardrobe."

Auntie had been a big star in Hollywood, so she had learned a lot about publicity. A few months ago she had started to use that knowledge to help other people. However, trouble followed Auntie around as much in real life as it did in her movies. (And I guess because we had the same name, it followed me, too.) Her first job had gotten us both involved with the theft of a priceless set of jewels called the Goblin Pearls. Things had gotten pretty hairy, but fortunately Auntie also had as much talent for solving a case in real life as she did in her films. We got the pearls back.

An excited Chinese woman came out of restaurant, ducking under the ribbon. "There you are, Tiger Lil," Ann Fisher said.

Ann was amazingly slender, considering the rich sauces and desserts she whipped up. Wisps of black hair hung from under her white chef's cap, and she wore a short white jacket that buttoned on one shoulder. It gave her a military look, which fitted her personality in the kitchen. In any other place she was as sweet as they come, but she ran her kitchen like a captain trying to save her ship from sinking in a storm.

Auntie put her hands on Ann's shoulder to guide her back inside. "You should be in the kitchen."

Ann held out a cell phone. "You got a call from Hollywood. They phoned your niece first, and she gave them our number here."

As Auntie took the call, Ann began to scan the crowd for her son. "Where's Barry? I want to wish him good luck." When she saw him, she beckoned him over. With an answering wave, Barry began to make his way toward his mother.

Barry's father, a tall man with dark-blond hair, came out of the restaurant. His vest was unbuttoned and streaked with flour, and the sleeves of his silk shirt had been rolled up past his elbows. I assumed he was serving as Ann's assistant in the kitchen.

"Barry doesn't need luck," Morgan Fisher declared proudly.

With him was his older son, Scott, my brother Chris's classmate. He was the star quarterback at Lowell and had almost won the city championship for his team. The sportswriters were calling him a blue-chipper who had the college coaches drooling. And after that he was a can't-miss prospect for the NFL.

Barry, who was five years younger, had always had to live in Scott's shadow. Everyone, from coaches to teachers to their parents, measured him against his brother. I felt really sorry for Barry. Just at the mention of his brother's name, Barry would tense up like a rubber band that had been stretched to the breaking point.

Scott studied Kong as he warmed up. "I don't know. Barry's competition looks as big and fast as a linebacker."

Suddenly Auntie let out a whoop that cut across the drums.

"What's up, Auntie?" I asked.

14

Auntie folded up the phone. "That was Clark Tom."

"You mean the actor from *East Meets West?*" Scott asked eagerly. "That show is in the top ten."

"Auntie met him at the Chinese New Year's parade," I bragged. (Clark had, in fact, come to my rescue when I had gotten into trouble because of my clunky costume.)

Auntie handed the phone back to Ann. "Clark was so impressed with me when we met that he's trying to get an episode written especially for me."

Ann dropped the phone into a pocket of her white coat. "Congratulations."

"He hasn't got the script yet," Auntie warned.

I elbowed Auntie. "Still want to concentrate on publicity?"

Auntie stared down at her prominent tummy and then groaned. "The camera adds ten pounds. I'll look like a blimp."

I wanted Auntie to be in the show almost as much as she did. "Just think 'Clark, Clark,' and go on a diet."

Auntie threw up her hands in resignation. "All right. I'll do it."

I'd heard that before. "Swear," I prompted.

Auntie shot me a dirty look. Lisa, my Hawaiian friend, would have called it "stink-eye." "Isn't my word good enough?" Auntie demanded.

"On most things yes, but you've been on eleven diets since you moved in with us. So swear."

"You're bossy enough to be a film director," Auntie grumbled, but she put up her hand. "But okay. So help me, Artie's beard."

When she swore by her agent's beard, I knew it was a solemn thing. And until now she had always avoided invoking Artie on her diets.

"Now don't do anything rash," Morgan teased. "We were counting on you to eat all the leftovers."

Auntie was caught in her own trap, sniffing mournfully at all the wonderful smells that the fan was wafting out from the restaurant's kitchen. "Well . . ." she said, already weakening.

I hooked an arm through one of hers. "And just to make sure you stay on your diet, I'm going to stay glued to you tighter than your shadow."

Auntie gave me more stink-eye. "You didn't get your mean streak from your mother's side of the family. It must be from your father's."

"Clark," I whispered to her. "Clark."

Auntie sighed and rapped a knuckle against her forehead in rhythm to the words. "Yes, Clark, Clark."

She was interrupted by a man shouting in a deep voice from the street. "What do you mean, you don't have change? What kind of cabby are you?"

CHAPTER THREE

I turned to see a Chinese man coming out of a taxi. He had shoulder-length hair that had been cut to frame his handsome face. And he was dressed all in black: shoes, socks, pants, turtleneck and raincoat. All his clothes had a designer look that didn't go with the pink cardboard box he held by a matching pink ribbon.

Ann Fisher looked as if she had just been slapped. "What is *he* doing here?"

"I don't know, but he looks like he doesn't trust your cooking anymore," Auntie said, nodding toward the pink box. "He came with his own food."

Barry finally came over and whispered in his father's ear. "Why on earth did you invite Uncle Leonard?" Morgan asked his son.

Ann looked at Barry, hurt. "To our opening—how could you?"

Barry said something in her ear.

"So what if he's my only brother?" Ann folded her arms as she watched her brother fight with the cabby.

17

"I didn't complain when we were kids and I did all the work in the restaurant and he got to study—though the only thing he was studying was a deck of cards. And I didn't complain when Dad died and left almost everything to Uncle Leonard. And I didn't even complain when he took most of the profits from the Ciao Chow."

"Well, it was his restaurant," Morgan pointed out.

"But we were the ones who made it a success," Ann countered. "And when we tried to leave, he said we couldn't go. He even brought in a lawyer who tried to bully us into staying."

"Your mother was the worst, though." Morgan winced.

"Mother always takes his side," Ann explained to Auntie. "And when we tried to open this place, Leonard scared every bank away from giving us a loan. I wound up having to put the whole building up for collateral."

Barry spoke into his brother's ear, and Scott nudged his mother. "Well, maybe it is time to make peace."

Ann patted Barry's cheek. "Tiger Lil, tell these two about Chinatown feuds."

"They can last a long time," Auntie informed the boys.

Uncle Leonard was clearly outraged, but the cabby—an old man in a cap with a visor—remained remarkably unimpressed. "Read the sign, mac." He pointed at the sign taped to a corner of one of the side windows.

It said in big, bold letters: NO CHANGE FOR BILLS OVER TWENTY DOLLARS.

"Surely you can make an exception in this case." Uncle Leonard briefly tried to turn on the charm as he thrust a hundred-dollar bill at the cabby.

The cabby leaned out the window. "Look, mac. The ride cost all of three bucks. Do I look like I carry the kind of cash to change that?"

Uncle Leonard looked down his nose. "Well, you should. I know the owner of this company, and I'm going to tell him how uncooperative you are."

The cabby didn't scare easily. "Yeah, well, when you see him, tell him I need new shocks too. This cab bounces more than a jumping jack."

Ann sighed. "Leonard's what happens when a rich Chinese family only has one son. The only one who ever said no to Leonard was me, and it took me six years to work up enough nerve."

"Come on, Mom," Barry coaxed. "New beginnings and all that."

Ann looked as if she was quite ready to let Leonard stew in his own mess, but then Barry leaned so close to his mom's ear that his mouth was practically touching it when he whispered to her.

Ann shook her head. "All right. I suppose it'd be nice if your uncle finally saw you dance. You can bail him out." She waved a hand at the restaurant. "You can get change for his hundred-dollar bill from the till."

Ann watched her husband and son make their way through the crowd to the cab.

Because of the drums, I couldn't hear what they were saying, but at least Barry was looking happy and hopeful.

Together with the cabby, Morgan, Barry and Uncle Leonard ducked under the ribbon and made their way into the restaurant. A moment later the cabby stormed back outside. "Cheapskate," he shouted over his shoulder. Then, to the rest of the crowd, he held up three dollar bills. "I don't even get a tip."

Uncle Leonard appeared in the doorway with a stormy expression on his face. When he saw Ann, he slipped under the ribbon and then charged toward her, waving one of the Wok Inn's red-leather menus over his head. "What's the meaning of this?"

"That's mine. You had no right to take that." Ann tried to snatch it from Uncle Leonard's hand, but he was too quick for her.

He waved it over his head. "I just checked it, Ann. You stole my menu."

"You can't steal what's already yours. I invented it for the Ciao Chow," she said angrily.

"I'm the one who invented it," Uncle Leonard snapped. "When you came to the Ciao Chow, you didn't know anything about French cuisine. You couldn't even tell a grenouille from ratatouille."

Ann glared at him. "The restaurant was going under until I came up with the dishes that made the Ciao Chow's reputation. And Morgan ran the place for you, so there was never any trouble. And since then you've scared away every restaurant that might hire us with your lawsuits. Well, not this time. This is our place."

Uncle Leonard looked irritated. He wasn't used to having anyone talk back to him. "Are you still spreading that rubbish around? Do I have to get a court injunction to stop you from spreading that slander?"

Ann jutted out her jaw. "I'm just telling the truth."

Outraged, Uncle Leonard shook the menu at her. "This is my menu." And then he waved it at the building. "And this is my building."

"Dad left it to me," Ann snapped.

"But I'm the oldest. It should be mine." He clutched the menu in both hands. "I'm going to shut you down as soon as I show this menu to my lawyer."

Ann planted her fists on her hips. "Fine. Have your lawyer talk to ours. They should know one another pretty well by now."

Morgan tried to play the peacemaker. "Come on, Leonard. None of us wants that."

"Stop it," Barry shouted. "Stop it!" He was so upset, he was almost trembling. "Can't you get together one time without quarreling?"

Everyone was so surprised to hear Barry speak out loud that they froze.

Uncle Leonard lowered the menu. He visibly fought to control his temper. "Truce?" he mumbled.

Ann hesitated and then nodded. "Truce."

Professor Sheng had noticed how upset Barry was and hurried over. With a nod to Ann, he said to Barry, "Time to warm up." Setting a hand lightly on Barry's shoulder, the Professor steered him back toward his classmates.

"You're going to make him into a basket case," Scott warned Ann and Uncle Leonard disgustedly.

Uncle Leonard studied his younger nephew as Barry began to warm up. "He's good, isn't he?"

"He got his light feet from our side, not Morgan's." Ann laughed.

Uncle Leonard pointed down at his feet. "Not these two hooves. He's got your agility. Just like Scott does." He clapped his hand on his nephew's shoulder. "I made quite a bundle on you last autumn."

"I developed quick feet because you were always chasing me," Ann said.

Uncle Leonard formed a *T* with his hands. "True enough, but why are there two lion dancers?"

"The lions dance through the maze." She indicated a small maze on the sidewalk constructed from short, squat columns, sawhorses supporting boards and heavy tables. Their legs were reinforced by sandbags.

"And the first one through gets to 'eat the lettuce.'"

The "lettuce" hung from the sign. It was a large ball of green hundred-dollar bills folded up to look like leaves. I'd heard Ann had spent most of her evenings this week making it.

"The lion dancer will then donate it to the On Lok Foundation," Morgan said. That was an organization that cared for senior Chinese Americans.

"Miss T?" Bernie extended a steaming Styrofoam cup of tea to Auntie.

"Thanks," Auntie said, taking the cup. "Oh, good. There's the deputy mayor. Go get him, will you, Bernie?" she asked, pointing out the Hispanic man getting out of a limousine.

The waitress almost saluted. "Right away, Miss T."

"Bernie's a real treasure," Auntie said to Ann as Bernie bustled off.

"I don't know what we'd have done without her," Morgan agreed.

Ann tapped her lip with a finger. "The odd thing is that I felt like I knew her the first time we met."

"Maybe she worked for your father," Auntie suggested as she sipped her tea.

"No, she says she never did," Ann said.

"In another life then," Morgan joked.

Auntie turned to me. "Go tell the schools that it's time to start, will you, kiddo?"

Trying to be as helpful as Bernie, I snapped off a salute. "Right away, Miss T."

CHAPTER FOUR

As I made my way over to Master Wang's group, Kong was watching Barry work out. "*He moves pretty good for a half-breed,*" Kong said in Chinese to his teacher.

I waited for Master Wang to reprimand Kong, but he said nothing.

My encounter with Kong had made me self-conscious about my Chinese, so I used English. "Barry is half Chinese," I corrected him, but Kong gave me a confused look, so I repeated myself in my broken Chinese.

Kong smiled in a superior way. "*He's still a mongrel.*"

That comment smacked of racism to me, and I expected Master Wang to correct his student. However, when again he said nothing, I wondered if Kong simply reflected the opinion of his teacher.

I fought to keep my temper as I said to him, "Master, my auntie would like to begin."

Master Wang ignored me, clicking his tongue and complaining to Kong instead. "*What's wrong with native-borns? All they can say is 'gulu gulu.'*" The nonsense words were meant to sound like English.

Cheeks burning with humiliation, I switched to Chinese—though I had to speak slowly and with careful enunciation. *"Please start, sir?"*

"Professor Sheng and I have already decided that he will get to warm up first, before the actual contest." He nodded curtly to his rival.

So I made my way over to Barry's group, where Professor Sheng was now standing and watching his student.

"Professor Sheng," I said politely, "would you please start the contest?"

"Certainly," he said. He gave a sign to a drummer, who nodded and picked up the tempo.

Slipping behind Barry, Akeem massaged his friend's shoulders briefly and then slapped him on the arm. "Go get 'em, tiger."

With a nod, Barry squatted, raising his hands as Akeem and a couple of other students lifted up the lion's head. It was just made out of bamboo and papier-mâché, so it was light enough, but it was bulky. As they slowly lowered it, Barry's head disappeared, and then his chest.

Akeem slipped under the cloth and began to move behind Barry as they warmed up.

Barry lowered the lower-jaw flap. I could see his face inside the head. He looked as if he had been swallowed by the lion. When Barry danced, he would be able to see only when he opened the mouth flap. Otherwise, he would have to look under the head's rim—all this while he pranced and danced like a lion. Bent over, Akeem could see nothing and would have to follow his friend's lead.

A short distance away Kong and his partner were also getting ready. When Kong lifted his lion's head up to his neck, I saw the muscles on his arms bulging. Poor Barry's looked puny in comparison.

When Barry stopped and Kong began, I could see the difference between the two styles. Barry's lion was playful in its majesty, but Kong's was the King of the Beasts. He stalked and prowled the sidewalk, a powerful hunter. Unfortunately, I had to admit that Kong's lion seemed more impressive.

Auntie took the microphone from Bernie. Catching my eye, she winked. It was show time.

"Welcome, ladies and gentlemen." Auntie's voice boomed over the speakers. If anyone in the city hadn't heard Auntie, it could only be because they were dead.

She nodded to the man next to her. "And thank you, Deputy Mayor Portales, for honoring us with your presence."

Deputy Mayor Portales reached for the mike to say a few words, but like the veteran scene-stealer she was, Auntie swung away so he grasped only empty air.

"On behalf of Ann and Morgan Fisher, I want to welcome all of you to the grand opening of the Wok Inn," Auntie went on cheerfully. "I'm Tiger Lil, your host for today." She waited for the applause to greet her name, but only a few people cheered.

For Auntie's sake I began to clap noisily. Quickly Professor Sheng joined me in clapping, elbowing the students next to him and looking all around him so that the others also joined in.

Auntie acknowledged her admirers with a graceful wave of her hand, and she went on. "Our lions are getting warmed up now, but when they're ready, they will have to dance through the Seven Challenges of the Warrior." She indicated the roped-off maze.

"The first one to get to the lettuce gets to eat it." She swung her hand toward the ball of hundred-dollar bills that hung from the restaurant sign. "There's two thousand dollars in that meal. And then the winner will spit it out into the hands of the On Lok Foundation." Auntie nodded her head at a Chinese American in a blue suit, who bowed to her in return. "That's Mr. Eng, who will receive it for them.

"So," Auntie announced with a big sweep of her hand, "let the festivities begin." Quickly she popped her earplugs into her ears.

That was Bernie's signal to set off the firecrackers that hung in strings from the sign on either side of the ball of money. As firemen watched from a fire truck a half block away, Bernie lit a match and held it first to one string and then the other. Then she beat a hasty retreat. The crowd waited expectantly. Bright flames ate their way up the strings to the first firecrackers.

They exploded with pops, and then, as the fire spread, more and more began to go off with loud bangs. Soon the air was filled with smoke. As the flames reached the ends of the strings, the smoke began to clear, revealing bits of bright-red paper drifting through the air. The doorway was already almost ankle deep in red paper.

There were strict laws against selling firecrackers in the city, but somehow Auntie had gotten hold of lots of them. (She had been very secretive about that, showing up one night with an armload of firecrackers.)

It was just as illegal to set them off, but Auntie had tackled city hall. I pitied the bureaucrat who tried to refuse her. The poor thing would have been flattened in a second beneath the Tiger Lil steamroller.

Dad had been so nervous about the firecrackers that he would not even allow us to store them in our house, because of the twin dangers of an explosion and a police raid. So we'd left them at the Wok Inn, coming down to assemble the strings that morning. It had been fun to tear off the bright-red tissue paper to free the fire-crackers, and to string their fuses together. I'd even saved a couple of the colorful labels.

The deputy mayor was looking dazed. My own ears were ringing; being this close to the exploding firecrackers was like being in the middle of a thunderclap. Auntie, though, looked as if she was standing in a peaceful, green meadow as she calmly popped the earplugs out of her ears again.

When she spoke through the microphone, she sounded like she was speaking underwater. "Lions, get ready."

The drummers raised their thick sticks, and then they began to pound on their great drums. It wasn't one of those elegant tattoos like in a Marine corps band. The rhythm instead felt like it was in sync with my own heartbeat, con-trolling my pulse.

Barry squatted and sprang upward, shaking the great head. Opening its mouth, he made the head roar silently. Barry and Akeem began to dance to the rhythm of the drums.

Barry in a lion's head was such a contrast to Barry in person. He was normally so shy that it seemed strange to see him prancing around in public. The funny thing, though, was that as I watched, I began to forget that it was my friends inside the costume. Instead, I felt as if I was seeing a real lion playing in its domain. Kong and his partner had begun dancing as well.

Once, on cable, I'd seen a real lion dance contest. Each contestant had imitated a lion, but on a small, flat screen it hadn't meant much. There had been no drums booming with vibrations so great that they passed right through your skin into your bones, and there was no nose-tickling tingle of gunpowder.

In that televised competition the contestants had been given points on style. However, the judges had had as much trouble scoring as judges do in figure skating, and the contest had ended in a big argument. Even so—and as loyal as I wanted to be to my friends—I had to admit that Kong and his partner were better.

Auntie's amplified voice cut across even the drums. "Lions, are you ready?"

Barry roared silently, his whole body shaking as he arched his head and opened the jaw flap. Kong did a series of squatting hops. And the drummer changed to a rapid rhythm.

"Get set," Auntie ordered.

As each lion tensed, the drummers picked up the beat to a frantic pace.

"Go!" Auntie said, and repeated herself in Chinese.

I expected them both to surge toward their courses through the maze, but both lions began to dance forward slowly, weaving and leaping.

Going over to Auntie, I tugged at her sleeve. "Why don't they just run?"

Putting a hand over her mike, Auntie explained, "Because they're lions. They have to stay in character, so to speak. Form is just as important as speed. I saw a lot of contests when I was in Hong Kong making kung fu movies. Jackie Chan did a lion dance in one film." Jackie Chan was a cross between Charlie Chaplin and Bruce Lee, and his movies were always packed when they played the Chinatown theaters. "Of course this contest isn't nearly as complicated as the one he was in. When you steal an idea, steal big, I always say."

With a leap, Barry and Akeem hopped on top of a table and began to dance there, circling and biting as if they were a starving lion. On his parallel course Kong and his partner did the same with just as much energy. They were the first to jump off, but when Barry and Akeem got down, I saw one of Kong's fellow students stick out a leg, tripping Barry.

Barry stumbled, falling to his knees, and Akeem tumbled over him. Instantly there were protests. I added my voice: "Hey, no fair. Foul!"

"*He tripped over his own two feet,*" one of Kong's schoolmates mocked in Chinese.

Professor Sheng raised a hand for silence. His face

remained impassive. Whatever Professor Sheng thought of the ethics of the other school, he kept it to himself. Each group began to encourage its own candidate once again.

I turned to Auntie. "Why did Master Wang let his student do that? It's not like they get to keep the money. Whoever wins has to hand it over to the charity."

"It's not money but the honor involved," Auntie explained, worried. She bit her lip. "I didn't think modern kids would get that involved, though."

I thought of Kong's contemptuous opinion of Barry. Perhaps his fellow students also thought of Barry as a mongrel. In that case, there was even more at stake here than pride.

In the meantime, though, Kong and his partner were already dancing their way through the lines of chairs that had been set up like a slalom course.

"Come on, Barry," Scott shouted clearly over the drums. He was used to making himself heard in hostile school stadiums. "Make us proud."

Barry sprang erect with new energy. When he momentarily raised the lion's head above his own, I could see the determined expression on his face. Behind him an equally determined Akeem was also getting to his feet. Barry said something to Akeem before he covered himself with the lion's head again. Akeem crouched over, bracing his legs. The next moment Barry leaped up onto the seat of the first chair.

I don't know if Barry and Akeem would have tried it a second time, but maybe their anger gave an edge to their concentration. Lifting the lion's head up, Barry raised a leg.

Professor Sheng was raising his hand to make them stop when Barry set his right foot on the back of the chair. And then, as the chair toppled backward, he used his momentum to swing his left foot to the back of the next chair. Akeem surged after him onto the seat of the chair and followed him across the chair's back.

There were over a dozen chairs, and they made each of them fall against the next like dominoes, walking across the chair backs as they did so.

At the incredible sight, Kong halted dead in his tracks halfway through his slalom. His partner blindly bumped into him.

As Barry reached the last chair, he jumped nimbly to the ground. And with a perfectly timed leap, Akeem landed behind him. They had reached the end of the course first. Their fellow students went absolutely crazy, high-fiving one another.

Lowering his jaw flap, Kong yelled angrily in Chinese, *"You're not supposed to do that! Cheat!"* He was so angry that the muscles stood out on his neck, and his whole body was rigid. Kong wasn't what I would call a good loser, especially when he lost to a "mongrel." Behind him his bewildered partner threw off the cape and stood up, looking around.

"Cheat! cheat!" Kong's fellow students took up the cry.

Defiantly Akeem started to shout, "Bar-ree! Bar-ree!" Turning around, he waved his arms at Professor Sheng's other students, who quickly joined in yelling their support of Barry.

Barry and Akeem stood beneath the lettuce, watching

Kong's shouting supporters edge toward them.

Fortunately, Master Wang was fairer than his pupils. Striding between the two angry schools, he called to his pupil, *"Kong, remember you are a lion. Behave honorably. You have lost. Cleverness is as important as strength."*

Reluctantly, Kong put his head back on while his partner got back beneath the cape. Then, as if his knees had suddenly grown rusty, Kong squatted among the slalom of chairs, bobbing his lion's head humbly and acknowledging the contest to Barry. And his partner followed suit.

"Bar-ree! Bar-ree!" his school kept shouting. Even Professor Sheng was yelling now.

With renewed energy Barry and Akeem began to dance, and then Barry climbed up onto Akeem's shoulders so that the lion seemed to be rearing on its hind legs.

Crouched on top of Akeem's shoulders, Barry made the lion head jerk and twist happily. He slowly straightened up, opening and shutting his jaw hungrily and proudly. He was reaching for the lettuce.

"He's got it," I yelped.

"All right, Barry!" Scott whooped exultantly.

It was almost as if Barry heard us through all of the crowd noise. Beneath the head, his legs tensed. The red lips spread wide, and he rose to take the tantalizing head of money. As the lettuce disappeared, loud cheers and applause rose from the crowd.

I couldn't have been prouder for Barry. "Did you see that? Did you see that?" Ann was asking everyone around her. Morgan was gleefully dialing someone on his cell phone.

I was glad for both my friends, but especially for Barry, who had been in the shadow of his star athlete brother. It was certainly my shy friend's moment to shine. And I went on shouting too.

CHAPTER FIVE

A s Barry and Akeem made their way through the alley to get to the back of the restaurant, Auntie poked Ann. "Better get ready for the presentation, kiddo."

Morgan had already gone inside the restaurant to get more firecrackers. Ann was searching for her brother as she went inside too. "Where has Leonard got to?" she muttered suspiciously.

In the meantime Auntie had raised her mike to advise the crowd to stay for the big finale. "You ain't seen nothin', folks. Stick around." Then she waved Mr. Eng over. It was time for the big firecracker finale.

"Such an exciting day," Mr. Eng enthused.

I left Auntie to exchange compliments with Mr. Eng while I hustled under the ribbon and into the restaurant.

Morgan was searching around frantically with the closed phone still in his hand, a box of assembled firecracker strings underneath one arm. "Where's the ladder?"

"Relax," I said. "The ladder's already outside."

"Yes, outside, yes," he said, running outside. I was afraid he was going to go right through the ribbon, but he ducked just in time.

It made me feel good to do an Auntie-ish thing as I hurried toward the kitchen. In the short hallway that connected the dining room with the kitchen, I nearly got knocked over by a man coming out of the rest room.

He looked like he was in his twenties, and he was wearing a short blue cotton jacket that had some florist's name on it.

"Watch it," he growled.

"Excu-u-se me," I said as I banged through the kitchen door. I used English, not caring if he understood or not.

After all the pandemonium outside, the kitchen felt strangely still and quiet. Huge platters of raw chicken and beef slices stood ready, along with bowls of freshly cleaned shrimp. Pyramids of uncooked won tons waited to be dropped into soup or to be fried and served with Ann's own hot, sweet Creole-style sauce.

Barry and Akeem were supposed to have brought the lettuce, all two thousand dollars' worth, here to the kitchen. I didn't see them, though.

But I saw Bernie putting a huge metal serving lid over a small silver tray.

I glanced around, eager to see two thousand dollars close up. "But where's the head of lettuce?"

Bernie tapped the lid. "Underneath here, Little Miss T. You didn't expect the lion to spit lettuce at Mr. Eng, did you?"

I laughed. "I guess not."

Then I saw a happy Barry trying to wipe the sweat away with a handful of paper towels. It must have been hot inside the lion costume; both Barry's and Akeem's T-shirts looked absolutely drenched, and Barry's hair was matted to his skull.

"Man, that smarts," Akeem said, examining his knees. His pants had been torn there where he fell, exposing nasty scrapes.

Barry whispered something to him, and Akeem glanced at the lion's costume. "We can't go back out in that."

Barry nodded.

I'd never seen such a big smile on Barry's face. He started to lean toward Akeem to reply, but caught himself. "It's funny, but I guess I feel more confident when I've got the costume on," he explained softly. "You know. Like a real lion." For most people it would have been a hushed kind of voice, but for Barry it was practically a shout.

"Then do it. Put it back on." I grinned.

From outside I heard a cheer as the deputy mayor cut the ribbon.

Akeem was just picking up the cape when Kong and his drummer friend stormed through the door. Looking at Kong's furious expression, I guessed he'd had second thoughts about conceding the contest. "*You can't push me around*," he said.

Puzzled, Barry turned to me for a translation, but Kong bulled straight into Akeem.

"Hey!" Akeem shouted, ricocheting off a large sink and thumping onto the floor.

With a shout Kong gave a little hop, swinging one leg around in a vicious kick that clipped Barry on the side of his head. Horrified, I watched Barry spin around like a top, straight into a table with a stack of shiny new pots.

Pots, table and Barry all fell over with enough noise for an anvil factory. I thought about getting help, but I didn't like the way Kong was closing in on Barry, who lay still among the mess.

Kong reminded me of a nature documentary Mom and I had seen once. She'd wanted me to avoid seeing violent cartoons, so instead she had forced me to watch a shark close in on a wounded fish for the kill.

Desperate for a weapon, I groped around a table until my hand closed on something. *"Leave alone!"* I shouted in Chinese as I ran toward him.

When Kong kept moving, I swung my weapon with all my might. *Splat!* A dead chicken bounced off Kong's shaved head. The packaged innards bounced out, plopped on his shoulder and then dropped to the floor.

As red juice dripped off his once-shiny dome, Kong turned toward me. I started to raise the battered chicken over my head, but I realized no one would ever be intimidated by the sight.

Slowly I started to back up. *"You heard Master Wang. You lose fair. You want me get him and remind you?"*

When Kong hesitated, I tried to follow up my advantage—though it was more like babbling. *"You not get away with this. Maybe he suspend you. Maybe even expel you."*

Kong fought to control himself, taking deep breaths. *"Don't you threaten me. You American-born think you're so* hot. But in Hong Kong you wouldn't survive a minute."

"Maybe, but you on my turf now," I reminded him, and over my shoulder I called to Bernie. "Get police."

"Right," she said. I heard the kitchen door swing shut behind her.

Kong got real nervous at the mention of the people in blue. Fear suddenly replaced his anger. "You think you've won, but you haven't. It won't end here."

I stepped between Barry and him, swinging the chicken back and forth. "I think it has."

"I'll remember you," Kong snarled, and he darted back out the door. I let out my breath in a large relieved sigh and let the chicken fall to the floor with a plop. In that documentary my mother had shown me, there had been a funny fish called a puffer fish that could blow up its body to twice its normal size to scare away predators. At that moment I felt just like that fish when it emptied itself out.

As I made a note to myself not to go down any dark alleys at night, I looked around for the drummer, unsure if a raw chicken would stop that beefy fellow, but I didn't see any sign of him. I figured he had made his exit out the front way. Uncle Leonard, though, was standing beside the money tray. "What's going on?" he asked, clutching his box.

"Your nephew ran into a poor sport," I said. "Where were you?"

"I had to make a call on the pay phone," he said. "Not that it's any of your business."

I ignored him as I knelt beside Barry. "You okay?"

With a groan, Barry sat up, pots clattering around him. "I think so," he said softly.

"Stay still," I said. Since Barry was all right, I headed over to Akeem. "How about you?"

He tried to lean back and winced. "Just some bruises, I think."

Morgan and Ann came in with Bernie. "Barry, are you all right?" Ann asked, running toward her son.

Barry nodded as he rose to his feet.

"Are you sure?" Morgan asked, staring at the pots now scattered all over the floor.

Nodding again, Barry helped Akeem to his feet. "We'll get them next time," Akeem swore.

Barry headed over to the lion's head.

Ann tried to fuss over Barry as he put the head back on. Akeem and I helped him. "Maybe we should go to the hospital, honey," she said.

As Akeem took his position behind him, Barry lowered the flap so he could look at his mom. "You're going to have to cook soon, Mom," he said softly. "You got the crowd. Let's pack them inside."

"We'll get him to the emergency room right after the presentation," I reassured Ann. Picking up the tray with the money, I followed Barry outside.

The drum was still booming, but the crowd was growing restless. Auntie looked relieved to see us. "You okay, kiddo?" she asked Barry.

For an answer, Barry began to prance, and Akeem began to dance behind him.

Snatching the mike from the deputy mayor, who was making another speech, Auntie waved a hand at Barry and Akeem. "Your lion's back."

The crowd cheered again as the drum played even more frenetically. I slid closer to Scott at the side, moving over to make room for Morgan and Ann. Uncle Leonard was again nowhere in sight.

In his triumph Barry swung around. When the jaw flap opened, Scott gave him a thumbs-up. "Great job," Scott said.

From the proud way Barry beamed, I think those two words meant as much to him as all the applause he had received. Taking advantage of the interruption, I slid in to give Barry the tray.

Somehow he managed to take the shining tray in one hand while he supported the head.

Lifting up her mike again, Auntie caught Mr. Eng's shoulder and pulled him in closer. "Mr. Eng, the Fishers of the Wok Inn are proud to present you with this ball of money, totaling two thousand dollars."

"Thank you," Mr. Eng said loudly. "This will be a double feast—a lunch for me and a generous donation for the foundation."

As Auntie stepped back, she motioned to the ever-present Bernie. "Get ready."

Bernie took out a book of matches and got ready to strike one. "Right, Miss T."

I glanced up nervously at the long, dangling firecracker strings. I took a couple of long side steps away from them as Scott held up the tray toward Barry.

"Bar-ree! Bar-ree!" Akeem started to chant again.

With one last prance Barry let the flap drop open. I could see he was grinning as he extended an arm out of the lion's head to give the tray to Mr. Eng.

And then the whole world seemed to explode.

A sudden ball of light blinded me for a moment, and then there was a huge boom as if a skyscraper-sized firecracker had just gone off.

I blinked my eyes a couple of times before I could see anything, and even then I saw little sparks. Horrified, I noticed scraps of burning hundred-dollar bills fluttering all around like fiery butterflies.

Mr. Eng was standing there with his arms stretched out in confusion, while Barry staggered around like a drunken lion. Smoke was coming out from under the lion head.

I stood there frozen like a dummy, but Scott had already reacted by dashing forward. The next moment he had disappeared beneath the lion, and both brothers crashed to the sidewalk.

The huge head split in two, and the lower jaw hung at a drunken angle like a broken window shutter while the two large goggle eyes bounced about crazily. Part of the muzzle had vanished, leaving a black-edged hole. Akeem was still standing, bent over under the cape.

There was silence as flaming fragments began to rain, and then chaos broke out. People began elbowing and shoving to get away before anything else blew up. At the same time, the people in the rear pushed forward to try to see what had happened.

Ann and Professor Sheng reached Barry and Scott at about the same time.

"Get back," Professor Sheng ordered his students. "And keep everyone else away. Help me," he said, struggling to widen the crack in the lion's head.

Ann added her strength to the professor's. With a loud snap, the head split in two. One half dropped onto the sidewalk while Professor Sheng and Ann held the other half. As they threw it aside, Barry's legs stirred, and we heard him groan. "Are you all right, honey?" Ann asked. "Can you move your arms?"

"Unh, yeah." Barry raised first one arm and then the other. "But . . ."

"But what, honey?" Ann asked anxiously. Professor Sheng hovered behind her, just as worried.

Barry's hand groped blindly for his mother. "I . . . I can't see."

CHAPTER SIX

Ann clasped her hand around his. "Somebody get an ambulance," she shouted.

In the noise I think hardly anyone beyond the front rank could have heard her. Then Auntie, coming out of her daze, held the mike up to her mouth again. "Will somebody call an ambulance? We have someone injured here."

Bernie fought her way to the front of the spectators. "I'll take care of it," she said.

"Please let her through, folks," Auntie said over the speakers.

Bernie didn't need help, though. Using her elbows in a way that would have done credit to a hockey player, she started back toward the restaurant. "Get out of the way," she kept repeating.

Professor Sheng stood up long enough to call to his students. "Keep this mob from growing," he instructed them, and I saw them hurry to obey.

In the meantime, Ann looked back at her son. "Can you move, honey? Scott is under you."

"Yeah." When Barry sat up, I could see the black powder marks around his eyes.

"Let me through. I'm his father," Morgan Fisher was protesting. He had made his way through the crowd, only to be stopped by Professor Sheng's students.

"Let him through," Auntie boomed, and the students moved aside.

As Ann held on to Barry, Professor Sheng drew the cape away from Scott. Scott groaned and blinked as the sunlight hit his face again, and he tried to raise his hand to shield his eyes. But then he winced.

"My arm," he said.

The head hadn't been that heavy, but perhaps he'd fallen in an awkward way. I thought of college football scholarships and a professional career going right out the window.

"You'll be okay," Morgan promised as he knelt beside his son. And he added his voice to those calling for an ambulance, but we could already hear sirens in the distance.

"Uh-oh." Auntie sighed as she saw the helmets bobbing toward us through the crowd. "The firemen's arms are going to wear out before they finish writing all the citations."

The firemen certainly didn't look as if they were going to ask Auntie for any autographs except on tickets. A fireman in a bulky black coat with yellow stripes stopped by Ann.

Kneeling, he gave both boys a quick visual inspection. Then he pulled a radio from his belt and listened to the scratchy response. "There's an ambulance on the way," he assured her. "I'm Captain Perone. Who's in charge here?"

"I guess I am," Morgan said.

Captain Perone craned his neck to take in the burning scraps of money and the red scraps of paper. However, he really only needed a nose to take in the stench of gunpowder. He glared at the deputy mayor. "We should never have let you set off those firecrackers."

Handing the mike to me, Auntie stepped forward. "That wasn't what blew up. It was the tray with the ball of money." Auntie indicated the burned tray. There was no sign of the lid.

The fireman must have worked the Chinatown area before; he knew what Auntie meant by the ball of money. He eyed the new strings of firecrackers that had hung nearby, then crouched to examine the tray. "You mean it exploded?"

"The money disintegrated, and the scraps burned." Auntie indicated the tiny bits of ash drifting about like gnats.

A new thought had occurred to Ann. "Oh, my. That was two thousand dollars. We'll have to make it good to the Foundation."

"You really don't have to," Mr. Eng assured her.

Morgan looked relieved. I was pretty sure they had used up most of their money on the restaurant. "Thanks."

Ann shook her head. "No, we really must insist on keeping our promise."

Morgan slapped his leg in frustration. "Why? It

wasn't our fault it was lost."

"She can't afford to lose face in Chinatown," Auntie explained to him.

Uncle Leonard suddenly appeared in the crowd. "Ann, if you need money, I'll loan it to you."

If Ann had not been holding on to Barry, I think she would have punched her brother. "So you can weasel your way into this restaurant too? No way."

Morgan glared at Uncle Leonard. "You've never wanted us to succeed. You've deliberately sabotaged every plan we've come up with. Did you have something to do with this?"

"It was you who sent the notes," Ann said accusingly.

Uncle Leonard still held his pink box. Maybe he thought it would protect him. "What notes?"

But at that moment Morgan jerked a thumb at the street. "The ambulance is here."

A huge, boxy ambulance with green stripes down the side had screeched up next to the fire engine. Its siren died, though the lights continued to flash.

"Tell Bernie to show you the notes," Ann said to the captain.

The paramedics swung out a gurney and brought it over. After quickly examining the boys, they put Barry on the stretcher. With a jerk of the handles, the stretcher rose to waist level so the paramedics could slide it into the ambulance. Scott and Ann climbed in behind him.

"Oh, this is terrible, terrible," Bernie moaned.

Auntie patted Ann on the arm. "You go to the hospital, kiddo. We'll handle things here."

"I'll take a cab, Ann," Morgan offered.

I thought of poor shy Barry. This had been his day to shine on his own, and then this had happened.

Professor Sheng had come over to the ambulance. "May I accompany you?" he asked Morgan.

Morgan lowered his head respectfully. "I'd be honored." Then he squeezed Akeem's shoulder, his eyes silently following the ambulance's progress through the traffic. "You want to go too, of course."

Akeem watched the ambulance scream away. "Please." It was the first time I'd heard Akeem use the word. Usually he couldn't see beyond his own belly button. It was a sign to me of how worried he really was.

Morgan took a ring of keys from his gray trousers and handed them to Auntie. "Would you lock up everything? I guess you'll figure out which is which."

"I'll catch you at the hospital," Uncle Leonard said, the pink box swinging in his hand. When Morgan looked at him in surprise, he said, "Barry and Scott are my nephews, after all."

"Whatever," the distracted Morgan said. I could see that Morgan didn't count on Uncle Leonard for much support.

I plucked at Akeem's T-shirt. "We'll join you later."

Akeem nodded, trailing his teacher between the cars to join Morgan as he hailed a cab.

As the taxi pulled away, Auntie sighed. "Those poor kids. In Chinatown you pay up if you owe someone."

Before Chinese New Year everyone tried to settle their debts. "It's not Ann's obligation, though."

Auntie shook her head. "I thought you were Chinatown enough to understand, but I guess you're not."

That stung. "I'm just as Chinatown as you," I insisted.

When Auntie realized she had hurt my feelings, she gave me a quick hug. "Of course you are, kiddo."

I knew it was silly, but I felt as if Auntie could fix anything. "Scott and Barry will be okay, won't they?" I asked, wanting reassurance.

"I hope so, kiddo." Auntie sighed. "But real life doesn't always have happy endings like movies do."

"Well, it should," I said.

CHAPTER SEVEN

"What happened?" another cop asked Captain Perone. He came striding up from the street onto the sidewalk. Everything about him reminded me of cubes—from his square jaw to his blocklike body. The hair on the sides of his head under his cap had been cut close, so it was almost like fine down. He introduced himself to us as Sergeant Moore.

"Ma'am, you want to come over?" Captain Perone called to Auntie. Then he told Sergeant Moore what had happened, leaving Auntie to fill in the gaps. This was one of those times when Auntie earned her publicity money—though I wondered if Ann and Morgan would have anything left over to pay her anyway.

Sergeant Moore let out a low whistle when she told him about the ball of money. "Two thousand dollars. That's a lot of coleslaw."

I noticed that Master Wang had slipped away, but Kong and his fellow students were packing up their lion head and drum in a pickup truck.

"Hey, you not leave yet," I shouted in Chinese.

"We're finished," Kong said.

"You stay. You talk police first," I said furiously, and then I said in English to Sergeant Moore, "That kid just tried to beat up Barry and Akeem. That could have just been a distraction for his pal to slip a bomb in with the money."

Sergeant Moore looked skeptical. "If he was already beating up your friends, why would he try to blow them up too?"

I remembered how furious Kong was. "He hated to lose to . . ." I couldn't bring myself to repeat what Kong had called my friend. "He said he would kill Barry. Kong hated Barry and Akeem. I wouldn't put it past Kong or those other bigots to take their revenge."

Sergeant Moore singled out one of the cops who was trying to control the crowd. I recognized him as Officer Quan, whom Auntie and I had met during the case of the Goblin Pearls.

"Quan, come with me," Sergeant Moore said. "I need you to translate."

Officer Quan nodded to Auntie and me. "You two are always in the middle of things, aren't you?" he asked as he accompanied the sergeant toward Kong and his fellow students.

"Ann mentioned threatening notes, too," Auntie said, glancing toward the restaurant. "Where's Bernie?"

Bernie was busy bringing the congratulatory pots of plants back inside the restaurant. "What do I do if someone comes in and wants to be served, Miss T? Mr. and Mrs. F left with their sons."

Auntie stared back at the empty restaurant. "I don't think that'll be a problem today. Maybe never."

"Oh," Bernie said. "Do you think the restaurant will close already?"

I felt sorry for her. I didn't know how many other jobs there were for a woman in her sixties.

Auntie slipped a card from her pocket. She kept a few with her at all times. "Here, Bernie. If that happens and you have trouble getting a job, you come to me. I've still got some friends around Chinatown. I'll get you something else."

"I'll do that." Suddenly she burst into tears. "It's very kind of you."

Auntie put her arm around the waitress and let Bernie cry on her shoulder. "Shame on me for feeling sorry for myself when those poor boys are going to the hospital," Bernie wept.

Good old Bernie. She might talk your ear off about her varicose veins, but she was still as sweet as they come.

"Do you know anything about the notes Ann mentioned?" Auntie asked, patting her on the back.

Bernie's shoulders lost their droop as she tucked the card away carefully in a pocket. "Yes, they started arriving last week. Do you think they're important?"

I realized that they might be. It might mean that the explosion was more than a spur-of-the-moment prank. Kong might not speak much English, but some of his friends probably did. And they could have sent threatening notes.

Auntie suddenly sounded like a veteran detective.

"Extortion's an ugly crime, Bernie. It hurts a lot of innocent people."

Bernie was old enough to have seen those movies in the theaters rather than on videotape, as I had. "Just like in *Hold That Tiger Lil.*"

That had been the first film in Auntie's famous series. In it she'd inherited a restaurant from an old boyfriend and then battled gangsters who wanted protection money. I'd noticed that people often mistook Auntie for the person she had played in the movies. The trouble was that sometimes Auntie couldn't make the distinction either.

Auntie looked grim. "Exactly."

"Then I'll get them right away, Miss T," Bernie said, and she went inside.

"Auntie," I said quietly, "this isn't like *Hold That Tiger Lil.*"

"No, it's more like *The Corpse Came C.O.D.*," Auntie said, turning to watch the sergeant interrogate Kong and his fellow students.

When Bernie came out with a manila envelope, Auntie opened it and took out a sheet of lined, yellow legal paper. Written on it in bold red letters were these words:

HONOUR THE DEBT! OR YOU WILL BE SORRY!

"They all say the same thing," Bernie explained, as Auntie took out others.

"What debt?" Auntie asked.

"Miss Ann didn't seem to know," Bernie said, scratching her head.

"Why didn't Ann tell me about the notes?" Auntie wondered.

Poor Bernie. She looked ready to cry. "Mr. Fisher wanted to go to the police, but she thought it was her brother playing a practical joke." She looked troubled. "But he wouldn't bomb his own nephews, would he?"

"He's got a temper," I reminded Auntie. "We both saw it."

"He might not have known Barry would be holding the money. Ann had to borrow money to start this place. She's in hock up to her ears," Auntie said.

I remembered what Auntie had said about the Fishers' having to make good the loss of the two thousand dollars. "If Uncle Leonard did this, he's trying to bankrupt her."

"Ms. Fisher threw the first couple of notes away, but when they kept arriving, Mr. Fisher started to save them." Bernie shook her head. "It's terrible. Terrible. Who would do a terrible thing like this, Miss T?"

My money was still on Kong and his street-rat friends, but Uncle Leonard was now a close second. Maybe the bomb had been tucked away inside that pink box he had been carrying.

"Better tell the long arm of the law, kiddo," Auntie said as she examined the other notes.

I approached Kong's group warily, expecting a battle when the sergeant hauled them off to jail. Kong was shifting his feet nervously as the sergeant questioned some of Kong's friends with Officer Quan's help. To my mind all of them looked shifty and guilty, so I was surprised when the sergeant told Quan, "They can go." Officer Quan repeated the message in Chinese.

Kong and his friends couldn't wait to climb onto the back of the pickup.

Trying not to shake, I cleared my throat. "Sergeant?"

Kong and his bunch glared straight at me. It was clear they blamed me for getting the police interested in them. I was going to have to be really careful walking around Chinatown after this.

Trying to ignore them, I gave the sergeant Auntie's message. However, I was careful to stay near the sergeant's bulky presence when we turned our backs on the gang.

As they pulled away, I whispered out of the corner of my mouth, "But he beat up Barry. You can't let him go."

"If I arrested everyone who got into a fight, there wouldn't be a Raiders fan in the county," the sergeant said impatiently.

"But what about Kong's friend, the drummer? He was in the kitchen, and he had time to slip the bomb beside the money," I said.

The sergeant closed his eyes as if in pain. "Did you see him do it?"

My personal opinion of the sergeant's detecting skills sank right down to the basement floor. "No, I was too busy watching Kong beat up my friends."

When we got to her, Auntie handed the notes to the sergeant. "These have been coming since last week," she said. "Maybe the explosion was part of an extortion plot."

He held the sheets by the edges. "And you handled them?" he asked in disgust.

Auntie waved a hand. "I've got small hands. See? That

means small fingerprints. I'm sure I haven't smudged the perpetrator's."

"Amateurs," the cop muttered as he studied them.

Bernie suddenly looked frightened. "Do you think it's the Powell Street Boys?" This was a gang that was still trying to carve out a turf for itself in Chinatown.

I wouldn't have put it past a street rat like Kong to be mixed up with them.

"Has anyone come by to ask for money?" Sergeant Moore asked.

"Well, no," Bernie admitted.

"The restaurant hasn't opened yet, Sergeant," Auntie pointed out. "How could there be money?"

"There was two thousand dollars hanging overhead," the sergeant said. "But if it was a gang, they would have taken the money, not blown it up."

Auntie nodded thoughtfully. "Maybe it was Leonard trying to ruin Ann."

Sergeant Moore put away his notebook. "It was probably some kids who slipped into the kitchen during the fight. They had a couple of cherry bombs and thought they'd play a practical joke, so they put them in with the money. Only they put too many in."

Suddenly I felt kind of funny. I'd been carrying the tray. It could have been me in the hospital instead of Barry and his brother.

"But the notes," Auntie said.

"We'll look for what prints are left." The cop glared at Auntie. "But it's probably just coincidence—some other kid playing a prank."

Auntie pursed her lips. "Well, maybe the explosion was set off by the other kung fu school because it didn't win."

Sergeant Moore laughed. "You've seen too many movies."

Auntie defended Hollywood. "Your problem is that you haven't seen enough of them," she said indignantly.

At that moment, from the corner of my eye, I caught a glimpse of something green fluttering across the sidewalk. All the money had burned up in that big flash of the explosion, except this one piece.

I'm always picking up souvenirs, so Mom says I'm a natural pack rat. When we visited Yosemite one time, my pants almost fell off because I had filled the pockets with so many rocks and sticks. I was only six at the time, but my family still jokes about it.

Instinctively, I snatched up the piece. Part of it was badly burned. When I held it up to my eyes to look at it more closely, the acrid burned smell made my nose itch.

"Get rid of it, kiddo," Auntie advised. "Something like that will only bring bad luck." Between Chinatown and Hollywood, Auntie was bursting with superstitions. "It's better to be safe than sorry," she added. It was her motto.

I held it out for Auntie to examine. "Look at this."

Auntie started to wave it away, but her hand paused in midair, and instead she leaned closer. "Why, it's a one-dollar bill."

I looked at it again to make sure. I saw only a number 1 and not 100. "What does a hundred-dollar bill look like?"

"Not like that." Auntie pointed at the bill. "That comes from right near George Washington's mug."

"So the ball of money that blew up was made up of one-dollar bills," I said, fingering the burned fragment. "But Ann made the lettuce with the one-hundred-dollar bills, and you hung it up this morning."

"Which means someone made up a second head of lettuce ahead of time," Auntie said, "and switched it in the kitchen."

I snapped my fingers. "And then blew it up to cover the theft of the real ball of two thousand dollars."

"So the explosion was more than a prank," Auntie said. "It was premeditated robbery."

Win or lose the contest, had Kong and his accomplice planned to steal the two thousand dollars all this time? I wouldn't have put anything past them.

The cop was unimpressed. "Will you put your Junior FBI kit away? So maybe Ms. Fisher decided to pad the ball of money by donating two thousand and one dollars to the charity."

"I'll ask her," Auntie promised, refusing to give up.

"You do that." The sergeant sounded bored.

Auntie was doing her best to control her temper. "You've got this case already neatly tied up with a ribbon and a bow, don't you? There's no need for more investigation. Or for paperwork."

"We've got real serious crimes in this city," Sergeant Moore said. "We don't have time for publicity stunts that go wrong."

"Publicity stunts," Auntie sputtered, but Sergeant Moore had already walked away.

I'd seen that look on Auntie's face in *Tiger Lil to the*

Rescue. She'd been a member of the jury who had refused to accept a prosecutor's case that had appeared just as neat and tidy. "I suppose it's silly to ask you to let the police handle it," I said.

"You heard the sergeant. They've already written off the case. Whoever hurt those boys is going to pay for it. No one messes with my clients," Auntie promised.

I told her about Kong and his friend and the fight in the kitchen. "I thought they might have set off the explosion for revenge, but maybe it was to cover up the theft. Maybe they had a bomb and a fake ball of money all set up."

She pulled at her lip. "So you weren't watching the drummer?"

"No, I was watching the fight, but maybe Kong did that on purpose to distract everyone while his friend made the exchange," I said.

Auntie's face wore the same thoughtful expression she'd had when tracking down a ring of master spies in *Watch Out, Tiger Lil.* "Who else was in there?"

"Well, Bernie, but she couldn't have done it," I said, thinking of that nice, helpful woman. "She wouldn't hurt a fly. But Uncle Leonard was there too."

"So that's where he was," Auntie said.

"He said he was making a call on the pay phone," I said. "Maybe he was just waiting for a chance at the money."

Auntie snapped her fingers. "Whoever wrote the note made a slip. In the note, honor is spelled with a *u* like the British do. So it couldn't be Leonard. It's probably someone from Hong Kong."

I remembered the surly delivery man. "There was a guy from the florist, but I didn't actually see him in the kitchen. I couldn't tell where he was from."

"Master Wang has a slight British accent, like some Hong Kong people do." Auntie looked suddenly thoughtful. "I couldn't talk you into going home, could I?"

My stomach began to twist tighter and tighter. "Aren't you going home too?"

Auntie raised her head with great dignity, as if she was a true lion. "I'm going to find out who injured my clients. In Chinatown you settle a debt—one way or another."

I remembered what she had said about Leonard and Ann, and suddenly I felt like an outsider. "Chinatown feuds run that deep?"

"And last a long, long time," Auntie confirmed. The way she said it made me shiver, as if someone had dragged an icicle down my spine.

"Where are you going to start your hunt?" I asked, already dreading the answer.

"At Master Wang's," Auntie answered. "If I find the money there, I'll have proof he or his students did it."

I thought of those drop-dead looks Kong and his friends had given me. "You're crazy."

Auntie squared her shoulders, as she had when the gangsters had her cornered on a rooftop in *Hold That Tiger Lil*, and then she shrugged and said her line before she jumped over an alley for a neighboring roof. "What the heck."

I couldn't let Auntie go alone—especially there among

mad bombers. Underneath her wisecracking exterior, the movie Tiger Lil had been a tough, determined woman. I guessed that the real woman wasn't that far apart from the film version. Maybe if I hung around my favorite great-aunt, some of that toughness would rub off on me.

I took a deep breath. "Then I go where you go."

Auntie gave me a hug. "I was hoping you'd say that, kiddo."

I still had that bad feeling in my gut. "But let's be careful, Auntie. You don't have stunt doubles anymore."

CHAPTER EIGHT

I had thought Master Wang's school would be in the old Chinatown, but it lay on upper Grant Avenue in what was technically the North Beach district—in what had been an Italian neighborhood in Auntie's childhood.

Ever since America had changed the immigration laws, though, there had been a population explosion in Chinatown. Because of the fair housing laws, a lot of Chinese had spilled over the old boundaries. Nowadays Italian delis and coffeehouses rubbed shoulders with Chinese music stores, and the mouthwatering smell of Italian salami mingled with that of Chinese sausage.

We crossed Columbus and walked along streets where gangs of Italian boys had chased Auntie back to Chinatown when she was a girl. Now groups of Italian and Chinese children played tag together. In fact, Master Wang's school was right next to pizza place that featured sweet-and-sour pizzas. Auntie sniffed the air appreciatively. "Maybe we should have some lunch."

That didn't sound like a bad idea, but I had to think

about Clark Tom. "You just said you wanted to go on a diet. Besides, this is no time to think of your stomach." I gave her arm a pinch.

"Well, look who took killjoy pills this morning," Auntie said, rubbing her arm.

I guess I'd been expecting some grand building like the martial arts schools in the kung fu movies, but Master Wang's school was just another storefront martial arts studio. They had popped up all over the city like mushrooms. Nowadays it seemed that half the city was taking some form of the martial arts.

Looking through the big plate-glass window, we could see the lion's head sitting in one corner along with the big drum. Except for that, the large room seemed almost bare. Blue mats covered most of the wooden floor. In one corner was a set of shelves. From floor to ceiling it was filled with trophies, testifying to the success of the school. A row of photographs of Chinese soldiers, all dressed in the same modern khaki uniform, hung high up on one wall. A curtained doorway must have led into the back.

It seemed ordinary enough, and yet I couldn't shake the feeling that something was weird. It was Auntie, though, who figured it out. "There's not one word of English," she said. She craned her neck back to look up at the huge sign over the studio. "Not even on the main sign." She grunted. "Let's find the back door."

We headed into a narrow side alley. It stank of old garbage, and I lost all thoughts of lunch. I didn't even like to think of what was squishing under my feet.

I jumped when I heard a rumble like thunder. "Sorry,"

Auntie said. "I knocked over a garbage can."

I put a hand over my racing heart. "Well, just be more careful."

"There's got to be a side door." Auntie's hands slid along the brick. "Ah, here it is. But it's so dim back here, I can't see the lock. Light one of these matches."

I heard her purse snap open, and I stood with outstretched palm until her groping fingers found it. "Careful with these."

I had to pull out a match and strike it by feel alone, but somehow I managed. In the flaring light I saw Auntie crouched over a doorknob. She had a hairpin in her hand. "This always works in the movies."

"To be specific, you did it in *Hold That Tiger Lil*," I corrected her, bending lower.

"That door was a prop one. This is real." Auntie hiked up her skirt before she crouched lower. "Now let's see. How did I do that?" she started to ask herself, when the door suddenly opened.

I gave a shout, dropping the match in my surprise. Auntie must have been just as shocked; the next moment she backed up blindly into me.

A man in a pizza parlor T-shirt slogged into the alleyway with a bag of garbage in either hand. "What do you want?" he demanded.

"We were . . . er . . . looking for the ladies' room," Auntie said, "and got locked out. Thanks."

"No prob," the pizza man said, and he went back inside. We followed him. At least we were in the building.

"We'll find it this time," Auntie said, and putting her

hands on my shoulders, she steered me inside into a long, narrow hallway. By the light of a single naked bulb, we saw huge hundred-pound sacks of flour stacked at the opposite end. The place smelled of rotten food, as if some of the garbage had escaped the pizza man's bags.

Auntie paused beside a curtained doorway. The fluorescent lights shone through the red satin, making her look as if she was bathed in blood. "Here's the studio."

I was ready to jump out of my skin. "Let's hope the money is here so we can leave."

Peering around the curtain, Auntie announced it was all clear. Then, walking on tiptoe, she slipped into the room beyond. I had to blink when I followed her into the room, just in time. I heard the outside door slam and the pizza man stumping back down the hallway.

Auntie was already examining the lion's head. "Check the drum," she instructed me.

That was easier said than done, because the skin of the drumhead was taut over the drum itself. For a moment, I thought I'd have to cut it open. However, I managed to shake the heavy drum back and forth. When there was no thump inside, I figured it was empty.

There wasn't much else in the room to inspect for the money except the photographs on the wall. I peered behind the back of the biggest, but there was nothing. When I had set it back, I stared at the face. "I've seen him before."

Auntie came up behind me. "Probably in the history books. That's Chiang Kai-shek. He was the president of China for years." Auntie surveyed the row. "All of these are KMT officers like Chiang Kai-shek."

"What's KMT?" I asked.

"KMT stands for the Kuomintang, the nationalist forces under Chiang Kai-shek. The nationalists fought the communists in China for a long time. Then," Auntie explained, "during World War Two, they joined the communists in fighting the Japanese Invasion. When the war was over, the nationalists returned to fighting the communists."

I thought of mainland China. "Obviously the communists won."

"Yes, and Chiang Kai-Shek and the KMT fled to Taiwan. Their big dream was to retake China from the communists." She studied the picture some more and then jerked her head at the curtained doorway. "Let's keep looking."

I felt exposed in the bright room with the plate-glass window, so I was actually glad to retreat to the safety of the dim hallway. We tried a few doors as we went along. The third door opened onto a staircase.

Auntie said softly to me, "Let me take the point. I'm the oldest. The oldest go first."

"No way. I'm quicker," I argued. "I can duck faster."

"But I'm smarter," Auntie said, and she plunged through the door first before I could stop her. The staircase had the same dusty, musty smell as the hallway, and the old worn treads creaked and groaned underneath our feet. And it was so narrow, we could go only single file.

The staircase led to a second floor. Another hallway ran from the staircase along the length of the building. Joining it at the middle was another hallway.

"They look like tenement rooms," Auntie said.

"Where do we start?" I studied the numerous doors in frustration.

"With the nearest," Auntie said, and she put her ear against one door. "There doesn't seem to be anyone in." She clicked her tongue when she rattled the doorknob. "Locked."

They were all locked. "Well, it's probably too late now, anyway." I sighed. "The money's probably in the bank."

"It takes a while to unfold and flatten that many bills," Auntie said.

"Yeah! It would call too much attention to bring it in as a lettuce," I realized.

"Exactly," Auntie said.

"Maybe it's time to talk to Norm," I suggested. Norm was Auntie's friend in the district attorney's office.

"Maybe." Auntie sighed.

As we turned around to go back down the stairs, a door suddenly opened, and Kong, his partner, and the drummer came out. Kong called back into the room in Chinese.

The next moment Master Wang strolled through the doorway. *"Leaving so soon? I wouldn't hear of it,"* he said in Chinese.

"We . . . unh . . . just got lost," Auntie said.

"How fortuitous. We can have a cup of tea together," Master Wang said.

Auntie clutched her stomach. *"No, really. I couldn't drink any more."*

Master Wang lost his smile. *"But I insist."*

CHAPTER NINE

He led us into a room that looked out on the street over his studio. There wasn't much furniture—just a desk in one corner and a heavy teak bench with red satin cushions in the other. An ornate teak bookcase was filled with files and books. There was a trophy on one shelf. On the desk sat a huge glass jar. Inside it, a fuzzy pancake swam in some kind of amber fluid. The only decoration on the wall was a photograph of a young officer in a nationalist uniform.

"*Please, be seated,*" he said in Chinese, and indicated the bench. Auntie and I sat down close together. I took comfort in the warm pressure of her leg against mine. Master Wang's students stood guarding the doorway.

Going behind the desk, he rolled out an old wooden swivel chair and sat down so he could face us. "Tea?" he asked Auntie in English.

"Really, no—" Auntie began.

"*Tea,*" Master Wang said in Chinese to the burly drummer with forearms like hams. With a bow, he left the room.

I glanced at the pancake again, wondering if it was a pet or a plant.

"You'll pardon me, but when I saw you earlier, you seemed familiar," Master Wang observed in Chinese.

"Auntie a famous Hollywood star," I said, hoping to impress Master Wang.

"I don't go to American movies," he said. *"I find them"*— he pursed his lips while he hunted for the right words— *"self-indulgent. Irresponsible."* He folded his hands over his lap. *"Rather like Americans."* When he said that, his eyes flicked toward me.

"And native-born?" I asked.

He smiled. *"Native-born are hollow bamboo. They're sealed at either end. Only good for drums."* He pantomimed thumping on one.

Behind him Kong and his partner laughed as they eyed each other. I wondered if the thumping was just a figure of speech, or if he sometimes turned his students loose on native-born.

"While foreign-born are branching bamboo," Auntie said.

Master Wang nodded, pleased. *"Open at one end to grow and grow—provided they can be kept pure."*

I thought again about the "purity" of Master Wang's way and wondered if there was room even for native-born Chinese. At any rate the two samples in front of us didn't look all that clean. In fact Kong's friend had a soy-sauce stain on the stomach of his T-shirt. I stared at it, but I had enough sense to keep my mouth shut.

Under my stare Kong's partner began to rub the spot

self-consciously, but he stopped when Master Wang looked at him. Then the master swung back toward us. *"I meant that you can continue to grow in a Chinese way only if you stay Chinese."*

"And yet America has so many distractions here," Auntie said.

"Only if you've got the money," Kong replied. *"Movies, video games, everything costs so much here. And if you don't speak English very well, it's hard to find a job."*

I didn't know Kong well, but I knew the expression. I could see it on the face of every person I saw washing dishes or emptying garbage or sweeping off a sidewalk. It was the face of someone who knew he would be doing crummy, low-paying work for the rest of his life.

"Don't speak out of turn," Master Wang scolded his student, and Kong made his face into a blank. Then Master Wang slowly turned around to stare at me. *"I suppose you think I'm a terrible bully,"* he said. I felt my face flushing; those were my exact thoughts. *"Have you ever asked yourself why these boys come to me? It's because they're beaten up by the native-born."*

The master was making me feel as if I was the guilty one. *"I have plenty foreign-born friends in school, and none of them gets beaten up."*

"And how much English do they speak?" he demanded.

"Better than I can speak Chinese," I had to confess.

He smiled in triumph. *"Exactly. But what about the ones who can speak only Chinese?"*

I scratched the back of my neck uncomfortably. *"They not be in my school. It magnet school only for top students.*

Students who have problems with English be assigned other schools."

"They aren't in any of your schools." Master Wang nodded at Kong and the other boy. "They drop out. I pick them up. I teach them to stand on their feet. If nothing else, I provide my students with pride. Kong lives with me."

"You don't pay the rent with just pride, though," Auntie said thoughtfully, fanning herself with her hand. And I wondered, too, how Master Wang paid for his school.

He rummaged around on his desk until he found a fan and handed it to Kong, who brought it over to Auntie. On the pink paper was printed the name of a bank in Chinatown. "My students and their families pay what they can. Some can afford higher fees than others. Some wealthy Chinese families still remember who and what they are."

"Thank you," Auntie said, taking the fan.

The master laced his fingers together. "I feel quite sure that I have seen you many years ago."

As she fanned herself, Auntie pointed to the framed photo on the wall. "You were in the KMT?"

When I stared harder at the photograph, I realized the uniformed officer was Master Wang in his early twenties, looking very scared.

The master looked at the photo as if it was the picture of a stranger. "We beat the Japanese, but not the communists."

"Perhaps we met in Taiwan," Auntie said. "A lot of nationalists fled there after the communists took over the mainland in 1948," she reminded me.

"No, I was part of the retreat to Hong Kong," Master

71

Wang said, emphasizing the word "retreat" rather than using "fled."

"*Business took me there too,*" Auntie said.

Master Wang wagged an index finger at Auntie. "*I'm sure I know you.*"

Auntie shut the fan with a snap. "*I should hope so. You're holding us captive.*"

Master Wang shook his head. "*I have seen you in the movies. But in Hong Kong, not in America.*"

Despite herself, Auntie preened. "*Which one?*"

Master Wang pursed his lips. "*It was a kung fu movie.*" The student in the dirty shirt tugged at master Wang's arm and then whispered in his ear. "*It was Kung-fu Granny,*" Master Wang said.

Auntie couldn't resist bragging. "*It made the most money of all my films.*"

Kong's partner whispered something else to Master Wang. "*And Killer Cook.*"

"*I quit that one when they demanded that I do a nude scene.*" Auntie frowned indignantly. "*They had no right to do what they did next.*"

Master Wang glanced curiously at Kong's partner, and he explained. "*They took a still picture of her face and super-imposed it over the head of some other actor who finished the scenes.*"

"*And the actor they used was twenty pounds heavier than me,*" Auntie protested. I wasn't sure what was worse in her mind, the nude scene or the extra fat.

Kong and his partner took a couple of steps backward together, giving her a wide berth. They huddled like timid vultures now, unsure whether to pounce.

"How much kung fu do you really know?" I whispered to Auntie in English.

"My stand-in knew everything we needed." She set the fan down. "Talk about bad wigs. They kept slipping off Rory's head."

Master Wang laughed. "That explains much." He switched to Chinese for Kong. *"You have nothing to fear from her."*

By then the drummer had returned with a tray. On it were a plain, heavy porcelain pot of steaming tea and two teacups.

At a gesture from the master, the drummer poured tea into the cups and then presented one to Auntie. *"We will drink to Hong Kong and its people. They won't be the first group the British betrayed. Now the communists have it all,"* said Master Wang.

"Why didn't you go to Taiwan?" Auntie asked.

The master frowned. *"In its greed to become an economic power, Taiwan has turned its back upon many of the party's principles. It seems intent upon becoming even greedier and more materialistic than America. And my comments have not always been appreciated there."*

That explained why he had come to America; even if he detested it, here at least he was free to complain about his hosts. I watched them sip. *"Lovely,"* Auntie said after the first taste.

"Dragon Well tea with pure spring water," the master said, sniffing the cup again.

"I wonder that you didn't get into movies," Auntie said.

"You're very photogenic."

"I was asked often enough, but I wasn't about to taint our heritage," the master said. "Why put all our secrets up on the screen where any fool can imitate them?"

"I know there were some masters who objected to having Bruce teach non-Chinese," Auntie said.

"Which Bruce was that?" the master asked.

"Bruce Lee," Auntie said.

My jaw dropped open. "You knew Bruce Lee?"

"I knew his father better," Auntie said, keeping her eyes on her tea, "but yes, I knew Bruce."

The master, though, was not impressed. He suddenly put his cup down as if he had lost his taste for it.

From behind her hand, Auntie whispered in English, "Actually, kiddo, I told him not to go into films. With his quick feet, I advised him to get into Broadway musicals as a dancer."

"Good thing you're not a casting director." I grinned.

Master Wang stood up brusquely. "Well, I really must thank you for helping me figure out why you are so familiar to me. It would have kept me up all night. Now we can get down to business."

I'd been with Auntie enough to know that it took a while for her Chinese clients to get to the point. "I suppose we should," Auntie said. She looked around and then set her cup down on the floor. The rim was now smeared bright red from her lipstick. "I was wondering what you knew about the lettuce."

"Nothing." The master smiled. "You have my word on that."

A master's word was not to be taken lightly, so Auntie reluctantly said, *"Well, since we have your word on the lettuce—"*

"You do," the master assured her.

"Then I think we'll just be leaving," Auntie said, and she rose from the bench.

"But first you must tell me what were you doing in our building," the master demanded.

"It's all my niece's fault," Auntie said. *"She got hungry. But when we went to the restaurant, we got lost trying to find the rest rooms."* She began shooing me toward the door like a hen with a little chick.

The master signed to the drummer, who jumped in front of the door. *"Our business isn't finished yet, madame."*

"And what business is that?" Auntie asked with a nervous smile.

"Sneaking about our building," the master said, and held up a hand before Auntie could deny that. *"And please don't try to offer your word. An actor's word is quite a different matter from a master's. You and your friends will have to provide an object lesson for others."*

"You'd beat up old woman and girl?" I asked angrily.

Even now Auntie was sensitive about her age. *"Who are you calling old, kiddo?"*

The master clasped his hands behind his back. *"From boyhood I have been fighting in wars so savage that there was no such thing as an innocent. As far as I'm concerned, I am still at war for the Chinese people. Whatever I do—however harsh— I do for them. When you snoop around like spies, you will be treated as spies."*

At his nod the master's students began to close on us.

The drummer pressed his fist into his palm as if he was especially going to like getting some revenge by drumming on hollow bamboo for a while.

CHAPTER TEN

As the Master's students started to crouch into their fighting stance, I looked around desperately for a weapon. Auntie coughed politely. *"If we've been challenged to a fight, whose rules are we using?"* she asked calmly.

"Mine, of course," the master said.

Auntie scratched the tip of her nose. *"Yes, but does that give us a choice of weapons? Under western rules we, as the challenged party, would get to choose."*

The master laughed deep in his belly. *"Madame, you can't really mean that. I was thinking of fists and feet, but let me assure you that my students know how to use most weapons, from spears to swords."*

"Let's cut out the minor characters," Auntie said, waving her hand to include the rest of us. *"How about you and me going head to head. What d'ya say?"*

The notion was so absurd that Kong's partner and the drummer started to laugh; Kong began to guffaw too. Even Master Wang lost his composure and started to chuckle. *"You can't be serious, madame?"*

"You bet," Auntie assured him.

"So you learned something from your stand-in." The master thought a moment. "Well, I suppose we could go down to the studio. While my collection is far from complete, it would have most of the basic weapons."

Auntie folded her arms. "I wasn't thinking of real weapons. I was thinking more of a test of strength."

Though the master tried to act as if he didn't care, I could see he was intrigued. Maybe it was just too easy for him to beat someone up. "And what is the nature of the test?"

"Do you accept the challenge?" Auntie demanded.

The master waved his hand impatiently. "Yes, yes."

"And if I win, you'll let us go free without punishment?" Auntie asked.

"Yes," the master said brusquely.

Auntie licked her lips and then tried to stretch a single into a triple. "And you will answer one more question?"

"All right. I'll be sporting," the master said as if he didn't think that was going to happen. "But what will you do if I win?"

"How about if I do free ads for the school?" Auntie asked. "As Kung-fu Granny, of course. Radio, TV, print. You name it."

"Only the vulgar advertise." Master Wang frowned. You'd have thought we'd asked him to put on a red clown's nose. "The best commercial in my viewpoint would be your own bruises and broken bones."

"How about a couple of cases of Lion Salve?" Auntie suggested quickly. The company that made the strong-smelling

78

medicinal rub was also one of her clients.

His students looked interested, but to their disappointment the master dismissed the notion with a wave of his hand. *"No. If you lose, we will return to my original plan. My students will turn you into an object lesson for all Chinatown."*

Auntie didn't seem the least bit afraid. *"Done,"* she said quickly.

With another laugh, Master Wang clapped his hands together. *"It's been a long time since I've found anyone so amusing."*

I couldn't see what Auntie was getting at. It seemed as if she was only prolonging the inevitable. We were going to get beaten up either right away or later.

However, Auntie strolled confidently over to the desk. *"I'll need two books."*

Master Wang made way for her. *"Be my guest."*

Auntie examined a shelf of books above the desk, moving from right to left and back again several times before she selected a small dictionary and a small atlas. Auntie held up one and then the other, studying each one critically. *"Yes, I think these will do."*

By now the master's students were curious. They started to crowd around.

Taking both books, Auntie went to a corner. "Shield me, kiddo," she whispered to me in English. At the same time, she turned her back to the master and his students.

Master Wang craned his neck, trying to see what Auntie was up to. His students, though, started to sneak closer.

I spread my legs and put out my arms, trying to be as much of a wall as I could. *"Hey, no cheat."*

Master Wang sat back self-consciously, trying to regain his dignity. *"Back,"* he said to Kong and the others.

They retreated to their former places but stood on tip-toe.

As I tried to be an obstruction, I stole a look over my shoulder. Auntie had set both books down on the back of the bench and opened them. Carefully, she brought both of them together and began to overlap the pages, one over another. "We can't rush this," she muttered, more to herself than to us.

When she was done, it looked like the two books were trying to devour each other. All their pages overlapped now.

"There we go," Auntie said, as if she had just success-fully baked a ten-layer cake.

Sliding her palms beneath the merged books, Auntie lifted them from the back of the bench. I stepped aside with a doubtful glance. I began wondering if I should make a dash for the restaurant. Maybe if I called the police right away and let Master Wang know I had done it, they would leave us alone.

Bearing the books upon her hands, Auntie marched toward the desk.

"What's this?" Master Wang asked when Auntie had set down the books on his desk.

Auntie stepped back. *"I challenge you to pull the two books apart."*

In his chair Master Wang rolled back over to his desk.

Studying the books from several angles, he set an elbow down on the desktop. *"Is this some kind of joke?"*

"There was a kung fu master who acted as a consultant for Kung-fu Granny," Auntie said. *"He called it his parable. One day he thought some of the actors were getting too rambunctious with their kicks and punches, so he gave them the same challenge."*

"A kung fu master?" Master Wang mused. *"This smacks of Professor Lin's humor."*

Auntie glanced at the ceiling as she tried to remember. *"I think that was his name. He liked to wear loud, red-checkered suits."*

"That's him," Master Wang said. All this time he had continued to study the books from various angles. *"He was the master of the five excellences, but he had the fashion sense of a turnip."*

"Is he still alive?" Auntie chatted on. You would have thought she was at her desk in Mom's beauty parlor.

Master Wang set his palms together as if in prayer as he kept examining the books. *"Yes, but I haven't seen him since I left Hong Kong."*

Kong whispered in Master Wang's ear. The master took a look at the books and then murmured something back. He and Kong held a whispered conversation for several minutes. In another moment Kong's fuzzy-headed partner had been drawn into the discussion. Only the drummer stayed in place like a guardian statue before the door.

Teacher and students pointed and poked and prodded the books from a variety of angles as if they were inspecting a bomb. Finally Master Wang laughed. *"This really does smack of Professor Lin. He was always coming up with some kind of trick like this at banquets."*

"So you give up?" Auntie asked.

"Let's play this out," Master Wang said, and he motioned to Kong.

Even though the challenge had been to Master Wang, Kong wasn't about to lose face. Kong took a book spine in either hand and then pulled. Though he wasn't as beefy as the drummer, he had a good set of muscles, so I expected the books to fly apart.

However, when they stayed together as if they'd been glued, Kong spread his feet apart and pulled harder. He pulled until his face was twisted into a grimace and his head had gone all red. Finally he lowered the books, panting openly.

"Give it to me," Kong's partner said, holding out his hands eagerly. He braced his feet against the floor and got a good grip on the two books. Then he began to yank at them. He tried that along several different axes—from left to right and from ceiling to floor and several other points on the compass. But he didn't have any more success than Kong.

"The books are witched," he puffed sourly.

"Here," the drummer called from the door, and he held out his hand.

Kong's partner took the books over to him. They seemed almost lost in the drummer's hands. I held my breath; I thought the drummer would tear them apart with one hand. He grunted and strained, his muscles bulging. Even the cords of his neck stood out. In the end he hung his head contritely. *"I can't,"* he confessed dolefully, and he returned the books to Kong's partner.

At a gesture from Master Wang, the student brought the books back to the desktop. Master Wang gave each book an experimental tug and then signed for Kong's partner to bring them to Auntie. *"What's the answer?"*

"I've asked several people for an explanation," Auntie said as Kong's partner held them out to her.

Opening the two books, Auntie began flipping the pages again, but this time she tried to keep the books apart. *"I've heard everything from capillary action to static electricity."* When she had separated about the books halfway, she pulled them apart. *"I just know it works."*

"Most educational," Master Wang agreed. *"Cleverness, not strength, is the key."* He looked at each of his students in turn. *"Do you understand?"* They all nodded respectfully.

"And if you learn something, you never actually lose," Master Wang rationalized. Again the nods.

"We go now?" I asked nervously.

The master signed to the drummer, who stepped away from the door. He chuckled. *"I can't wait till the next banquet. It should humble some of these so-called professors a bit."*

Auntie motioned me toward the door, and I moved gratefully toward it. However, Auntie herself lingered. *"I also get one question."*

Master Wang had begun flipping the pages, merging the two books again. *"This is really more of a parlor trick than a challenge."*

"*You still gave up,*" Auntie pointed out.

Master Wang wasn't used to having people call him on such points, but he sighed. "*That will teach me not to negotiate. What is your question?*"

"*I'm going to ask you again. Did you or any of your students hurt Barry and steal the money?*" Auntie asked.

Master Wang looked puzzled. "*The money was destroyed in the explosion. What do you mean, steal?*"

So Auntie told him about the one-dollar bill that I had found.

I sucked in my breath along with the students, and for a moment I waited for Master Wang to explode. However, he glared at Kong instead. "*Do you see what your failure has cost us? People think we are the thieves and the bombers.*" I guessed that, as the head, Kong was more responsible than his partner.

Kong bowed his head quickly. "*I'm sorry, Master.*"

"*Will apologies restore our reputation?*" Master Wang demanded.

Kong looked sick. He glanced at his master and then away again. He didn't dare to speak.

Master Wang turned to Auntie. "*No, we did not steal the money. Nor did we set the bomb.*"

"*Do you know who did?*" Auntie asked.

A smile spread slowly across his face. "*That's two questions.*"

I was ready to bolt for the door, but Auntie was always a gambler. "*I thought you were worried about the reputation of your school. Until the real culprit gets caught, people are going to suspect you.*"

Master Wang considered that for a moment, drumming his fingers on one of the books. *"Do you remember the white carnations that were in a pot at the restaurant?"* he finally asked.

"No," Auntie said, *"I was busy, but I would've remembered them if I had seen them. They'd be in poor taste."*

I glanced at Auntie, hoping for an explanation, but she was concentrating on the master.

Master Wang went back to playing with the books. *"Exactly. Clearly someone didn't wish your clients well. I saw the flowers when they were delivered. I'd ask the florist who sent them. Maybe then you'll know who really has a grudge against the Fishers."*

I remembered the delivery man I'd bumped into. Maybe he'd been behind the extortion notes. If only I could remember the name on his jacket. But what was wrong with white carnations? I wondered.

"Well, thanks," Auntie said, and then in English she said to me, "Come on, kiddo. We're heading back to the Wok Inn."

I opened the door and stepped into the hallway. I didn't think that dingy, ugly place could have looked more welcome. As I waited on the threshold for Auntie, though, Master Wang suddenly whipped up a leg. Before I could cry a warning to Auntie, the leg shot out and kicked Kong instead.

As Kong fell at Auntie's feet, Master Wang said sternly, *"What kind of lion are you? In China we put lions outside of temples to guard them. They defend our ways with courage and conviction; but because of your failure, you have caused our* reputation to become stained instead. *People now think we are thieves and worse. Don't come back until our name is clean again."*

Lying on the floor, Kong rolled over and pulled himself up to lean on one elbow. *"But how, Master?"* he bleated.

Master Wang clicked his tongue. *"A true lion would help these two find the real thief."*

Kong stared at us doubtfully. *"These two?"* I think he would rather have carried around two filthy pigs on his back.

Master Wang folded his arms. *"Though I don't know what a fool like you could do."*

Kong sat up, looking ready to cry. Neither the drummer nor Kong's former partner gave him much sympathy, though. It was Auntie who bent and took his arm. *"Come on,"* she said.

He shook free of her and stood up. He glanced desperately at his master, but Master Wang had started reading one of the books on his desk, and Kong's fellow students were doing their best to ignore him.

He almost ran from the room. I hopped out of his way quickly. He took a few steps down the hallway and then just stood there miserably.

I started to feel sorry for him and hunted for some words to make him feel better. *"Thanks for help,"* I said.

He gave himself an angry shake. *"It's all your fault,"* he snapped.

Just as Auntie neared the doorway, Master Wang called out, *"If you come to snoop around again, remember: I won't be fooled by a parlor trick next time."*

"Let's hope it never comes to that," Auntie wished fervently in English as she joined us in the hallway.

"Amen," I muttered.

CHAPTER ELEVEN

Auntie and I breathed a sigh of relief when we got to the sidewalk.

"*It true what you say before?*" I asked Kong. "*You not get job?*"

"*What do you care?*" Kong shrugged.

I had assumed that all the foreign-born Chinese were like my friend Linda. She got better grades than me in everything, including English. If what the master said was true, though, Kong would never be able to get good wages speaking only Chinese. No wonder he was so angry sometimes. I would be too.

"*I sorry if true,*" I said.

Kong looked as if he agreed with Master Wang that native-born were empty-headed. "*You can't do anything about it.*"

"*I still sorry.*"

Kong's eyes flicked over Auntie's round shape doubtfully. "*Were you really a famous film star?*"

"*She is famous star,*" I corrected him. "*You should see

Hold That Tiger Lil."

"*Never heard of it,*" Kong said.

I have to say that I hadn't really known much about Auntie's movies before she had moved up here to San Francisco. But since then I'd seen as many of her movies as I could. Still, my Chinese just wasn't up to bragging about Auntie. "*You miss good stuff,*" I said.

Auntie added, "*Most of my movies were before your time.*"

I wasn't about to give up, though, without one last shot. "*You owe to yourself. See movie where Chinese American is hero.*" Even as I spoke, I thought I was beginning to sound like my brother, Chris.

Kong just shut himself off. It was like watching a Chinatown store closed up for the night when the door of corrugated iron comes down. "*I'm Chinese,*" he said, "*not American.*"

"*You can be both Chinese and American,*" I said. "*Look at Auntie. She native-born, and she both.*"

"*Who cares, anyway?*" he said sullenly.

"*Obviously you don't,*" Auntie said.

"*That's right.*" On his long legs he strode away from us.

I thought he was such an idiot that I started to open my mouth to shout something after him. Auntie put a hand on my shoulder, though. "Take it easy on him, kiddo. He's hiding a lot of hurt."

I thought of what Master Wang had said. "You mean from Americans?" I said, glad to be switching back to English.

"And native-borns like me." Auntie stared at the stiff

back with the broad shoulders. "And he's probably heard things from some Americans who were just as foolish."

I punched the air. "I'd like to pound sense into every one of them."

"Then you'd be playing their game," Auntie gently reminded me.

Kong had stopped at the corner, but he refused to turn around. His whole body was tense. I supposed his world would be easier if it was all one big studio floor where he could pound an opponent into submission.

Thinking about Kong made me think about my friend Barry. Maybe there was more than one reason why Barry had joined Professor Sheng's school. Maybe it wasn't just to bang a few heads, like Kong. "Is that why Barry is so shy?" I asked Auntie. "Is it because people pick on him because he's part Chinese and short?"

Auntie shrugged. "Maybe. It'd also be hard enough living up to his big brother's achievements, without all the other stuff going on too."

"Barry's always going to be part Chinese, and he looks like he's always going to stay short," I said. "So do you think he's going to be shy forever?"

Auntie shrugged. "I think he's found the answer in lion dancing. He found something Chinese he's comfortable with, and his height isn't a problem when he dances. There's all sorts of evil spirits around. Some of them are on the outside, and some of them are on the inside. And maybe he dances to drive them all away."

Kong had jammed his hands into his pants pockets. As he heard us come up behind him, he asked without turning around, *"Are you feeling sorry for me? Because if you are, the last thing I want is your pity."*

We let the little grouch walk a couple of steps ahead of us until we reached Columbus. It was nearly rush hour, and traffic had picked up. There were buses and cars edging up on the crosswalk, ready to shoot across the intersection at Columbus and Broadway any moment. The traffic was flowing along Broadway in a river of brightly colored steel. During rush hour Chinatown felt more like an island than ever.

The restaurant was locked in the front, with all the plants moved inside into a circle, like a herd of yaks forming up to hold off the wolves. On the door was a sign hand-lettered in English on the back of a sheet of paper that had once announced the opening of the restaurant—I recognized it because I had done the flyers myself in the Xerox shop. The words were written in pencil in large, perfect letters: CLOSED UNTIL FURTHER NOTICE. I assumed Bernie had done that.

Auntie peered through the big plate-glass window, her breath steaming up the window. "I think there's a light on in back."

So we moved into the narrow side alley, walking on the dirty bricks. I couldn't help wondering if they had been there since the old days of Chinatown.

The door to the kitchen was open, and the kitchen was spotless and shiny. Bernie had scrubbed everything. At the moment she was having a cup of tea at a small table. She seemed shocked when she saw us. "You look awful, Miss T."

"If I was a cat, I'd be on my ninth life now," Auntie

said, sinking onto a nearby chair. Kong hesitated in the doorway, but Auntie waved him over to another seat.

Bernie got quickly to her feet to surrender her chair to me. "There's plenty of food. Let me get something out of the fridge and heat it up."

Auntie perked up at the thought of Ann's treats. "That could be just the medicine I need."

"Remember Clark Tom," I reminded her, taking a seat.

Auntie gave me another stink-eye look, but then she shook her head. "Got anything healthy?"

"There's carrots," Bernie said, going over to a bowl of them on the counter. The carrots had been sliced to look like orange coins. She shuffled back on tired feet and held it out to Auntie. "Customers have been coming by and looking in the window the whole afternoon."

"We'll get things straightened out," she tried to assure the waitress. "And then the restaurant can open."

Auntie began to munch unhappily on a handful of carrots. Fortunately Ann had cut up a lot of other vegetables, which we ate raw. Every now and then I looked longingly at the refrigerator and wished Bernie could heat something for me. However, I had to be good for Auntie's sake.

"So what's the word from the hospital?" I asked.

"Both boys are going to be okay," Bernie said.

"That's good news," I said.

"You bet, kiddo," she said, standing up. "So let's check those plants."

Bernie looked surprised. She caught Auntie's wrist. "What do the plants have to do with anything?"

"Master Wang thought the florist might provide a clue to the real robber." Auntie suddenly pointed at someone hurrying out the front, carrying a plant. "Hey! Drop that plant." She tried to jerk free, but Bernie had a tight grip on her.

"What's wrong, Miss T?" Bernie asked.

Bernie might be sweet, but she was awfully stupid. Kong had been sitting there, not understanding a thing, but when he saw me jump to my feet, he got up as well. And when I bolted through the door into the front, Kong was only a step behind.

The door stood open to the street as a man in a short blue cotton jacket was trying to get out. I dove toward the man's legs, wrapping my arms around them.

"The plant!" Auntie cried in alarm as it flew out of the thief's arms

Letting go of the thief, I rolled onto my back. For the sake of my reputation, I'd like to say I caught the pot of carnations, but it was more that my stomach served as a cushion for them to land on. "Whoosh!" I said as it drove the breath out of me.

In the meantime Kong threw himself onto the thief, but he had more desire than weight. He couldn't keep the thief from getting up on all fours. Suddenly Kong looked like he was riding a wild bronco. The bouncing made him sound as if he had the hiccups.

"*I-I-I g-got you,*" he insisted in Chinese.

I flung myself at the thief, my shoulder hitting his rear end. The force was enough to knock him back onto his stomach. However, the outcome of the battle was still in doubt until Auntie came over and calmly sat on him.

"Who invited you, kiddo?" she asked the thief.

I got to my knees and examined the black characters written on the red ribbon on the pot. I spoke Chinese better than I read it, and recognized only the usual words for good fortune, but not the others. *"Any threats?"* I asked, showing the ribbon to Kong and Auntie.

Kong frowned in disgust.

"They're awful," Auntie said as she examined the flowers.

The carnations looked a little sickly, but not awful. I said so.

"These flowers are white," Auntie explained. "And in Chinese tradition white is the color of mourning." She caught hold of the pot, dragging it closer toward her. "You send white flowers to a funeral, never to a celebration. These were probably sent by the same person who was sending the extortion notes."

"So maybe the florist could lead us to the thief."

The pot itself had been wrapped in red foil. "There's no card," Auntie said, disappointed.

Suddenly Bernie gave a high-pitched shriek and fell on the floor. She must have come in.

Auntie, Kong and I got to our feet. "What's wrong?" Auntie asked.

Too late, I realized no one was paying attention to the thief. He staggered to his feet and started to run.

"I'll get him," Kong shouted.

The thief turned in the doorway, and Kong suddenly

stood there as if his feet were glued to the floor.

"*I get him,*" I said.

Kong, though, couldn't let me beat him. He stepped in front of me, forcing me to stop. "*That's my job.*"

As the thief plunged through the doorway, Kong followed.

"Be careful," Auntie called after him.

I took Bernie's arm. "You okay?"

"The thief scared me," Bernie said apologetically as she sat up.

"I should have stayed by your side," Auntie said guiltily. "You're not used to handling criminal types."

Auntie held the pot out toward Bernie as I helped her to her feet.

"Do you remember who brought it?" Auntie asked Bernie.

Bernie was in tears. "I've got a run in my support hose." She showed us the jagged gash in the black nylon.

The poor woman. And she didn't have any tips or wages to buy new ones. Auntie felt just as sorry for her. "I'll get you a new pair."

"I don't take charity," Bernie said, rubbing her knee. "But I'd like some answers. What's this all about?"

Setting the pot on the table, Auntie filled her in on our trip to Master Wang's. She finished with saying, "So he tipped us off about the carnations. He knew something."

Bernie rubbed her forehead as she stared at the flowers. "There were so many deliveries today."

Kong came back at that moment, panting. "*I lost him*

on Broadway. He cut right across the traffic that had the green light," he said.

I thought of the dense river of vehicles. "*He made it to other side?*"

"*He was shiftier than a snake,*" Kong said testily. "*I tried my best.*"

"*Why you just stand there first?*" I asked.

Kong just shrugged.

I switched to English. "How did he get in here?" I asked Auntie.

"He must've picked the lock somehow," Bernie said.

Suddenly I looked down. There were a half dozen small red cards. "What's this?" I picked one of them up.

"They must have fallen out of his pocket when he fell," Auntie said, holding out her hand.

I passed it on hopefully. "Can you read this?"

It was all Chinese characters in gold. "It says Bright Circle Garden Florist," Auntie said.

I recognized the name. "That's Uncle Errol's place," I said. "He plays cards with Dad and Mom every Saturday evening."

"We'll never get anything out of that cheap jerk." Auntie sighed.

"You've played cards with him too?" I asked Auntie.

Auntie chuckled and did a little dance with me. "I taught him the box step, kiddo. He promised to take me to the movies in exchange, and he never did."

"Is he from Hong Kong?" I asked, remembering the British spelling on the extortion note.

"No, he's a true-blue native who was born here,"

Auntie said. "But I wouldn't use spelling to rule out anyone. A native-born could use that spelling to throw us off the track." Turning to Bernie, she asked her to lock up after we left.

CHAPTER TWELVE

Auntie didn't want to take Kong and me with her, but I wasn't about to let her go to Uncle Errol's alone.

"You need your bodyguards," I said, glancing at the card. "*Where this?*" I asked, showing it to Kong.

"*You wouldn't know the address,*" he said. "*It's in a little alley.*"

It was clear he regarded me as an outsider, though I lived only a few blocks from Old Chinatown and my parents had been raised here. I started to bristle, but then remembered he couldn't speak English. He surely couldn't read it. It couldn't be easy for him to go very far from Chinatown. "*I guess I too busy going around rest of San Francisco,*" I bragged.

I couldn't tell whether it was my words or my smirk, but it was Kong's turn to glower. We just seemed to be like oil and water.

"Quiet in the Peanut Gallery," Auntie said, clapping her hands.

She led us up a street of apartment houses for a couple more blocks, and then she brought us to the mouth of an alley. After the sunny light of the street, the alley seemed like another world. It was as dim as the forest floor of Muir Woods, where the tops of giant redwoods form a green roof far overhead. But instead of ancient trees, there were old buildings of brick or stone. Fire escapes wound up their fronts like vines, and overhead were television antennas like bare dead branches.

I'd been down plenty of alleys in Chinatown, but they'd seemed alive with people sounds—babies crying, kids shouting. This one was dead quiet.

Auntie plunged right into the alley, though.

I pressed nearer her. Even Kong took a step closer.

We moved down the gloomy alley. The buildings here couldn't have been any taller than four stories. And yet because the alley was narrow, they seemed taller and menacing. I felt as if eyes were watching me all the way.

Auntie walked in a kind of strut whenever she was in Chinatown and was feeling like she was on her old turf. The strut made her look like a little bantam rooster. Head up. Cheerful. Confident. Ready to take on the world.

She stopped in front of a store with a large painted sign overhead, but the plate-glass window had been boarded up and painted over. Somebody had put out some leafy potted plants, but otherwise there was nothing to show that it was a florist's shop.

However, when Auntie opened the door, warm, moist air rushed out. The place was like a greenhouse. The shelves and tables on either side were so crammed with plants that there was only a narrow central aisle. We had to walk single file.

At the back of the store was a counter, and to its right was a huge refrigerator. I could see all sorts of flowers through its glass doors. A girl in a pink smock sat on a stool, fussing over a vase of flowers. "Yes?" she said.

"I'm looking for Errol," Auntie said.

"Mr. Errol isn't here," the girl said, picking up scissors.

"Tell him Tiger Lil is here," Auntie said.

The girl snipped at a leaf. "I told you, he's not here."

There was a yellow curtain over a doorway behind the counter. The next moment it jingled back on its rings. In the doorway was the man I knew as Uncle Errol. He had a receding hairline and double chins. In his hand he had a racing form.

Barreling around the counter, he stopped and bent his legs, leaning back as he thrust out his arms dramatically. "Lil! Need more firecrackers? I just got in a fresh shipment."

So this was the source of Auntie's firecrackers. I wondered if my parents knew about Uncle Errol's side business.

Instead of hugging him, however, Auntie took one of his hands and began to shake it. "Not today."

Errol seemed hurt. "I thought you'd gotten over my broken promise when you came to see me last time. What was it now?"

"You heard about what happened at the Wok Inn?" Auntie interrupted him.

Uncle Errol frowned. "The explosion; yeah." He shook his head in what seemed like genuine sorrow. "Kids nowadays. They just don't know how to use fireworks."

I waited for Auntie to correct Uncle Errol and bring up the matter of the thief from his shop, and the extortion notes. That's what she might have done outside Chinatown. But I'd hung around with her enough to know that she conducted business a little more slowly in Chinatown, chatting about this or that with a person. Once, after being bored for a half hour by small talk, I'd asked her why she hadn't gotten to the point sooner.

"They would have thought me rude," Auntie had explained. "And they would have been right."

I supposed it was just another way that I was empty inside like bamboo. At any rate, it didn't surprise me terribly when she pointed to me. "Look who's helping her old auntie today."

"You brought Lily," he said with delight.

"Hi," I said.

"And this is Kong," Auntie said, introducing him.

Uncle Errol's took in Kong's martial arts costume. "You're so famous you need a bodyguard now?"

As they chatted, it started to feel as hot and humid as a jungle inside that shop. With all those plants, there should have been plenty of oxygen, but it was so warm that I started to feel drowsy.

Finally Uncle Errol leaned on the counter and jerked his head toward me. "You look like Ah Mock," he said to me.

"Who?" I asked Auntie.

"My father," Auntie explained.

"I never met my great-grandfather," I said.

"Well, he ran a little noodle shop. No one ever went hungry when he was around," Uncle Errol said, and glanced at Auntie for confirmation. "Right, Lil?"

"If a kid didn't have the money for a meal, Dad'd give him credit," Auntie agreed.

"There were a lot of hard days when my stomach was empty. I mean, so empty it was flat as a pancake." Uncle Errol stretched across several plants, not caring what he crushed, to grip my shoulder. "I'd never have made it without your great-grandfather."

"He probably fed half of Chinatown," Auntie said.

"But if you thought you could cheat him and sneak out without paying . . ." Uncle Errol's hand suddenly became a fist. He stopped just short of hitting me. Instead, his knuckles barely grazed my chin. "*Koosh!* He'd make you see stars."

I tried to smile despite the fist hovering next to my cheek. "More effective than a bill collector."

Uncle Errol opened his fist and gently brushed my cheek with his fingers. "He was too soft a touch. There's a lot of people never settled their debts with him. Chinese style, you're supposed to settle your debts every New Year's."

"This is a lot better than leafing through an old photo album," I said. Uncle Errol was being so nice now. It didn't go along with what had just happened in the restaurant, though.

"Then you come by anytime." Uncle Errol beamed. "I'll tell you all about him."

"I'd like that," I said, "but . . ."

Uncle Errol picked up something in my voice and stiffened. "But what?"

Auntie was shaking her head. She wanted me to leave things to her, and maybe if I'd been more used to Chinatown and how they did things here, I would have. However, I was as impatient as any American—which is to say I had no patience. "Why did you send someone to steal the flowers from the restaurant?"

Auntie sucked in her breath; so did the girl at the counter. Kong looked puzzled, because we were using English. However, instead of exploding, Uncle Errol pressed a hand against his chest. "Why would I do that?"

I was beginning to feel sorry that I hadn't let Auntie handle it. "You sent a pot of flowers to the opening."

"Of course I did. My first job was with Ann's father, washing dishes," Uncle Errol said indignantly.

Auntie cleared her throat. "But why send white carnations? They were half dead, Errol."

"I never sent those." Perplexed, Uncle Errol turned to the girl. "Get me the book."

The girl pulled a ringed binder from behind the counter. Each order had been recorded on its own page. Intently, Uncle Errol flipped through the pages until he stabbed his finger down triumphantly. "Ha, there it is. I sent red carnations."

We squeezed around to look. Someone had written in a bold, slanting hand: a dozen red carnations, going to Ann's restaurant.

"That's not what came." Auntie told Uncle Errol about the events of the day, ending with the story of almost catching the thief. Then she held up the little stack of business cards. "He dropped these, Errol."

Uncle Errol took them, his finger flipping back and forth across the edges thoughtfully. Then he called to someone behind the curtain, "Lung?"

Lung swept the curtain aside from the rear doorway to reveal a storehouse. "*Yeah?*" he asked in Chinese.

There, in the blue jacket, was the flower thief.

CHAPTER THIRTEEN

"You!" This time I didn't wait for Kong but dove for the thief myself.

It was like trying to tackle a bull. He started to drag me along as he charged around the counter and toward the doorway.

"*You won't get away this time*," Kong said, and he threw himself at the thief. However, the clumsy idiot landed on me instead of on the thief. Together we fell to the shop floor.

Auntie tried to grab the thief, but she wound up holding his blue jacket as he raced right out of it and through the door. By the time I got disentangled from Kong, Lung was heading out of the mouth of the alley.

I gave Kong a shove. "*You no help.*"

"*I was trying.*" Kong sulked.

Uncle Errol was standing outside his shop. "*And don't you come back,*" he shouted, his big voice booming in the alley. "*You're nothing but an ungrateful ——.*" And he added some swear words, some of which I had heard on the street and others that were new to me.

Auntie helped me to my feet. "You okay, kiddo?"

"*I would be, except for this jerk,*" I said, nodding to Kong. I used Chinese on purpose.

Kong got up, dusting himself off. "*Watch it.*"

"*Or what? You trip over your two big feet,*" I snapped. "*Go back to master.*" Kong stood there embarrassed. Too late, I remembered that he couldn't. "*I—I sorry,*" I stammered.

He ignored me.

Uncle Errol came back, spreading his arms out apologetically. "I'm so sorry. You try to give a kid a break, and look what you get—nothing but trouble."

"What sort of break, Errol?" Auntie asked.

"He came to me with this song and dance about how he wanted to quit the Powell Street Boys. All he needed was a job. And I believed him. Well, I guess a leopard can't change his spots," Uncle Errol said.

"So you think the Powell Street Boys are behind the explosion plot?" Auntie asked. That was bad news.

Uncle Errol thought about that for a moment. "Naw, the Powell Street Boys would trash a place and then empty the cash register. They wouldn't use bombs."

Auntie folded her arms. "So maybe Lung was acting on his own."

"It's a faster way to get money than delivering flowers." Uncle Errol sighed. "I'm hurt, though, that you thought it was me."

Auntie put her hand on Uncle Errol's shoulder. "I'm sorry, Errol. How about that dance you owe me?"

"Irma," Uncle Errol said to the girl behind the counter.

Irma obligingly turned the volume up on the radio. It was a slow tune, and in that narrow shop all they could do was a simple box step. Errol moved gracefully, and Auntie . . . well, she just seemed to float. Both of them shed years, until I could see them as a young couple dancing on a shiny nightclub floor by candlelit tables.

When the music ended, I clapped, and Kong, who had been watching curiously, joined in.

"Thank you, thank you." Auntie dropped a curtsy, and Uncle Errol took a bow.

"Those were the days, weren't they, Lil?" Uncle Errol asked wistfully.

Auntie nudged Uncle Errol. "You should have come with me to Hollywood." She added to us, "Errol was quite the dancer in his prime."

"And still am." Uncle Errol smiled sadly. "But where can a guy and a gal go dancing nowadays? I'm not ready to hop up and down with a bunch of kids."

"I heard about a hotel that has tea socials," Auntie suggested.

Uncle Errol clasped Auntie's hand. "Then let's go."

"You got a date," Auntie promised, "once I help Ann get back her money."

"That's a job for the cops," Uncle Errol said.

Auntie shook her head. "They won't help. It's something we've got to do on our own. Do you know where Lung lives?"

Uncle Errol looked over his shoulder toward the counter. "Irma?"

Irma disappeared in the back and came out with a file, which she handed to Uncle Errol. "For what it's worth, this is the address he gave me." Uncle Errol wrote it down on a receipt and handed it to Auntie. "Just be careful."

Auntie folded it up and put it in her purse. "I will, Errol. I want to go dancing."

When we headed out of the alley, I told Kong what had happened. Then we turned east, moving down the steep hill. A battered white van gunned its engine, pulling away from the curb. It smelled of fish. I held my nose as we passed it. It was waiting for a space in traffic.

Kong didn't seem bothered by the odor, though. He badgered Auntie. *"It's no use going there. He's probably run away."*

"He'd have to pick up the money first," Auntie said. *"Maybe we'll catch him."*

"Scared?" I asked Kong.

Kong stiffened. *"Only for you two."*

"This time we not one who let him get away," I said.

Auntie held her hands up in the shape of a T. *"Time out, you two. We're all on the same team. Right?"* she asked in Chinese.

"Yes," I mumbled.

Kong nodded.

"Sorry," I said, and I waited. When he didn't apologize in return, I prodded him. *"Well?"*

"Well, what?" Kong said.

"You supposed apologize back," I said.

Kong tilted back his head. *"My first year here I kept saying, 'Sorry, sorry, sorry.' But it was for no reason. No one*

108

explained things to me. They just laughed when I made mistakes."

"It sounds like they're the ones who should have apologized," Auntie said sympathetically.

"Auntie," I said, surprised that she was taking his side.

"Think how it'd be if we went to China," Auntie said. "Wouldn't we make mistakes too?"

"I suppose," I said grudgingly.

The noise didn't help my mood any. The van was crawling at about five miles an hour and was now about thirty feet behind us. I could hear the old motor rumbling. And behind it a long line of drivers began hitting their car horns in frustration.

I figured the driver was just another delivery person who was looking for an address, so I didn't give the van a second thought.

"I come to this country because everyone is equal," Kong said. "But when I get here, all I find are people who want to use you. They pay less than minimum wage, and when you object, they tell you go find another job, but you can't."

"Because you can't speak English," Auntie said.

The frustration poured out of Kong. "It's one big trap. The landlord takes all your money. You can never save. And you can never get sick."

"You not have health plan?" I asked, shocked.

Kong gave a bitter laugh. "There are two Americas, one for my kind and one for the rest of you."

"The employer pays someone like Kong under the table," Auntie explained. "There's no such things as benefits or a vacation."

"It's like being a nail and everyone pounds away at you." Kong pretended to swing a hammer.

The honking got louder.

Despite myself I found myself sympathizing with Kong. "No reason be American, huh?"

Kong couldn't resist getting in another dig. "And then you have some native-born looking down her nose at you."

"Huh—and China-born look down nose at me," I said.

Kong opened his mouth for a reply, but then he shut it. He didn't say any more as we followed Auntie, but he looked thoughtful as we started to cross the street at the intersection.

Suddenly I heard a sickening crash and the tinkling of glass. "It sounds like a car crash," I said, thinking that a car had finally rear-ended the van.

I turned just in time to see the van bounce off a parked Volvo. The impact had smashed in the van's fender and left a huge dent running along the side. Car alarms began shrieking, and air bags inflated.

And then I realized that the van was picking up speed as it moved down the steep hill straight toward us—and there was no one at the steering wheel!

just stood there and watched the van get bigger and bigger. My mind told me it couldn't really be happening.

"*Get out of the way,*" Kong yelled.

I felt a powerful shove between my shoulder blades—as if someone had struck me with a two-by-four—and I went flying toward the sidewalk. Even though I put my hands out in time, my palms hurt as the sidewalk charged up at me, and I scraped my knees.

Beside me I heard Auntie give a grunt, so I assumed Kong had shoved her with his other hand. But what about Kong?

I rolled over in time to see him dive through the air. The van roared past like a white whirlwind. A mother with a stroller barely got of the way, a truck driver honked his horn angrily, and then there was a horrendous crash—like someone had dumped a bin of metal parts and glass.

Kong landed on the sidewalk, but his shoulder hit the street sign. For a moment he just lay there.

It's a lot easier to dislike people when they're just jerks.

It's hard to carry on a feud with someone who's saved your life. Why did Kong have to go and complicate everything by being brave?

"Kong?" I pushed myself up on my forearms. Auntie was rolling over, groaning.

Kong lay still. I tried to get to my feet but could only sit.

A man with a bag full of partially plucked ducks stopped running long enough to ask, "Are you all right?"

"Yes, but—" I was going to tell him about Auntie and Kong, but the man had run on to gawk at the accident. A small crowd had already gathered around the van. Its front had caved in against the hood of a poultry truck in the intersection. Otherwise it might have kept going straight down the hill and into the bay.

The poultry truck driver didn't look hurt, but the crash had sent a whirlwind of white feathers into the air, so it seemed to be snowing in the intersection.

Even as the driver took a couple of tentative steps, chickens began escaping from the broken cages on the truck's flatbed. "My chickens," he said in dismay, as they began to fly and leap from his truck.

A dozen of the spectators raised their hands to try to catch the chickens in midair, but the birds flapped out of their way. Others tried to catch the ones that landed on the street. I saw one lady snag a chicken and hide it in her paper shopping bag. The other chickens scooted in all directions. Between all the shouting and the squawking, I barely heard the sirens.

Eventually I saw a half dozen firefighters hurry up,

their black coats flapping. The yellow stripes made them look like bumblebees. "Get back," one of the firemen began shouting. "The gas tank could go."

The spectators at the back of the crowd were close enough to hear him, and they backed away.

I poked Auntie beside me. "Auntie?"

She rolled onto her side and winced. "It's been a while since I did an action flick. How about you?" she asked, sitting up.

"I'm okay, but I don't think Kong is." I got to my feet painfully. Nothing seemed broken, but I could feel bruises and scrapes that would keep me up tonight.

"I knew there was some good in him," Auntie said smugly.

I had to admit that Auntie had been right. I felt ashamed of all the bad thoughts I'd had about him. "Kong?" I asked again as I knelt next to him. When I tried to roll him over, he cried out in pain.

"Where it hurt?" I asked.

"My shoulder." He grimaced. He sat up and punched the pole of the street sign angrily.

When he winced, I couldn't help saying, *"That stupid."*

He shook the injured hand in the air. *"You're telling me. I should have realized we were being followed."*

I thought he was being paranoid like Master Wang. *"No one follow us. Driver of van maybe look for address."*

"The driver was waiting to send it after us," Kong insisted.

"What makes you think that?" Auntie asked.

Kong struggled to put his thoughts into words and gave up. *"It's just a feeling."* He shrugged.

It took the firefighters a while to clear the scene. By then everyone but the truck driver had stopped trying to catch the chickens. All eyes were turned toward the van and the truck in anticipation of a huge Hollywood-style explosion. Though I couldn't actually see the street where the van was, I could smell the gasoline, and the firemen had begun spraying foam from some portable canisters.

I saw a man and a woman in blue jackets and pants walk by holding medical kits.

"Over here," I said in English, pointing to Kong.

Kong shook his head. *"I don't have the money."*

"We'll handle it," Auntie promised.

I helped interpret while the medics examined Kong. "Nothing broken or dislocated. I think it's just a sprain, but we should get some X rays."

"No," Kong said when I told him what the medics had said. He got to his feet hurriedly.

"Relax, Kong. We'll pay for the costs."

"No hospitals, no police," he said, starting to walk away.

The medics hesitated, trying to decide if they should follow him. However, at that moment one of the firefighters began shouting for the medics to come and check out the truck driver.

"Wait. Please take care of . . . of my friend," I said finally. Kong's heroics had made me willing to try to see things from his view. If I'd been treated the way he had, I might be angry and suspicious all the time too.

However, when I turned to look for Kong, he was gone. "Kong," I shouted.

Auntie grabbed my arm. "He said no police, remember?"

"I wonder what he's hiding," I said.

"Maybe he's already got some kind of police record," Auntie suggested. "Or maybe he's here illegally. But whatever it is, he's too young to have those kinds of secrets."

I saw some police worm their way through the crowd. After talking to the firefighters, they began to question people. I saw the medics point toward us. When Officer Quan saw who it was, he brushed some feathers from his clothes and walked up to us. "Well, well, well. I should've guessed you'd be behind this. What are you going to do for an encore? Burn down San Francisco?"

Auntie gave him a lopsided grin. "Only if I can film it." And she told him about the runaway van and the crash, leaving out Kong. "Funny, but we never saw the van driver."

"We already called it in." Officer Quan indicated the walkie-talkie clipped to his shoulder. "The van was stolen just a little while ago."

Auntie thought about that. "So the thief panicked for some reason."

"Something like that," Officer Quan said, watching idly as a hen strutted by.

"Or someone was stalking us," I said, remembering Kong's suspicions. First he'd used a bomb. Now he'd tried to run us down.

"Why would someone steal a van and try to run you over with it?" Officer Quan asked.

I thought of Lung. We'd exposed his little extortion scheme. Maybe he wanted revenge. However, Officer Quan just laughed when I told him. He had no more imagination than his sergeant. "Look. You got lucky with the pearls, but don't let it go to your head. This Lung sounds like some small-time hood. Not a clever extortionist." He walked away.

"But the money is missing," I protested.

"We don't have time to track down every wild story," he said over his shoulder.

I took a deep breath, but Auntie put a hand on my shoulder. "Remember: When you argue with a cop, the cop always wins."

I let my breath out slowly. "Well, what do we do? Look for Kong?"

"He'll find us if he wants to," Auntie said. "Let's check out Lung's address."

We headed down the steep slope. It was a good thing that the van had stopped when it had, or it could have been moving at the speed of light by the time it reached the foot of the hill.

As we passed by an optometrist's office, Auntie looked into the window, which was was filled with glasses in all shades. Auntie pointed them out to me with a chuckle. "The doctor hasn't changed his window display since I was your age."

In Portsmouth Square a few elderly men were playing chess at the concrete tables, and a few graying women sat on benches chatting, though most of the spectators had gone up the hill to see the accident.

When we crossed Kearny, Auntie got out the slip of paper with the address again. She held the paper at arm's length as she tried to study it. "What's it say?" she asked, squinting.

It was pure vanity that kept Auntie from buying reading glasses. "Don't you think it's time to visit the eye doctor?" I jabbed a finger in the direction of the optometrist's office.

Auntie swung the paper over toward me. "And what if a casting director should see me with glasses? No more sweet, innocent ingenue roles for me. So all this dieting would be wasted."

Auntie was as far away from ingenue parts as I was from becoming the President of the United States, but I merely pointed out the obvious. "Who's going to read to you when I'm in school? Or are you going to ask total strangers?"

Auntie drew herself up indignantly. "You're as young—and slim—as you feel. You just have to think positive."

I knew better to argue with Auntie when it touched on her film career, so I just told her what the address was.

To our left a hotel rose high into the air. To our right was a row of tenement houses. They squatted there like so many elderly, tired pigeons. However, though we walked back and forth along the block, there was no building with that address.

"I should have known—a fake address." Auntie crumpled up the paper in disgust.

"*I could have told you it wouldn't do any good,*" Kong said.

I turned and saw him. I guess he had been watching us from the hotel to make sure we weren't being followed.

"*You read English?*" I asked.

"*No,*" Kong said defiantly, "*but you don't have to read much to recognize an address. I'm not that stupid.*"

He might have saved our lives, but he wasn't making it easy to like him. Before I could say anything, though, Auntie got to the point. "*Did you see who was driving the van?*" Auntie asked. "*He tried to kill us.*"

Kong looked at Auntie as if he thought the question was ridiculous. "*It was an accident.*"

"*You not think accident before, and cops tell us van stolen,*" I said.

"*It was?*" Kong grew pale.

"*I think whoever stole it tried to kill us,*" Auntie said. She started to lean back against the brick wall but realized how dirty it was.

"*You have to give me time to talk to him first. I can get him to give himself up,*" Kong insisted.

"*You know the thief?*" Auntie asked.

A muscle worked on the side of Kong's jaw as if he was grinding his teeth. "*It was my brother, Lung.*"

f he hadn't just saved my life, I might have kicked him. I started to count to ten. Even Auntie, who had been defending him just a while ago, took several deep breaths. Kong shifted his feet uncomfortably.

"*So you let him escape back at the restaurant,*" she finally said.

Kong straightened defiantly. "*He's my brother.*"

I fought to keep my voice even. "*He thief. He hurt two boys.*"

Even now Kong tried to defend his brother. "*You have to understand. He didn't want to join the Powell Street Boys. But he couldn't speak English. He got sick of the lousy jobs in Chinatown. And once he got in with them, they changed him.*" He gazed at the passing cars. "*He steals cars for them.*" He waved a hand at the street. "*He can take any van in a minute. I guess now he's into other things too.*"

So one brother was in one of the worst gangs in San Francisco. The other had followed the opposite path and signed on with Master Wang, who might be a bully and a bigot but seemed honest.

"*You saw him behind the wheel?*" Auntie asked.

Kong shook his head. "*No, but it must have been him. I figure when we got too close, he decided to cover up his tracks.*"

"*With couple tons van,*" I said. "*He try kill you. You his brother.*"

Kong shot me an angry look, but he didn't try to deny it. "*We made him feel trapped.*"

If he had been the least bit apologetic, I might have sympathized with him, but he was being pigheaded and arrogant, so I went for the jugular. "*Master Wang understand what you do? Your brother cast blame on his school.*"

The blade had gone home. Suddenly Kong's shoulders sagged. I guess all that arrogance had just been a show, like a mask hiding what he was really feeling.

Kong swallowed. "*I'm prepared to be expelled.*"

The school gave Kong his pride and identity, but he was willing to give it up for his brother. I was impressed, even if he was a surly street rat.

Auntie put her hand on my shoulder. "*Easy. Kong didn't have to save our lives.*"

Kong sighed miserably. "*He's gone too far. He shouldn't have tried to kill you.*"

"*He try kill you too,*" I said.

"*He shouldn't have tried to do that either,*" Kong admitted, as if he still couldn't believe it. "*I can't protect him anymore.*"

Auntie held up the fake address. "*Do you know where he really lives?*"

"Let me talk to him first," Kong begged.

"Why we trust you?" I asked suspiciously.

Kong licked his lips nervously. "You can watch from outside. If he runs, call the police."

I thought he wanted to warn his brother and help him escape. "Only one way out?" I asked.

"You can check the building," he said stiffly.

"Your record not great," I snapped.

"One way or another, we'll put an end to this matter," Kong promised. "I'll keep my word."

Auntie gave a little shake of her head as a sign for me to stop antagonizing Kong. "What makes you think he hasn't run already?"

Kong spread his arms helplessly. "He might have, but I doubt it. He'd never leave Father's journal behind. It's all we have."

"Your father dead?" I asked.

"And my mother," Kong nodded. "They were trying to hold down two jobs each. They barely had time to sleep. The hard work killed them."

"Did you have any other family over here?" Auntie asked.

Kong suddenly looked embarrassed. "No. My brother and I are on our own."

Auntie clicked her tongued sympathetically. "That kind of isolation must be rough. There's a lot of people in Chinatown who would put the blame on you."

"Why?" I asked Auntie in English, wondering why Kong would appear so ashamed. "Kong and his brother can't help being poor."

Auntie explained, "The problem isn't the fact that

121

they're poor. It's that they're orphans. And it doesn't sound like they have any extended family either: no aunts, no cousins, no grandparents. For a Chinese, that's the worst thing. There's no one to protect you. No one to stay with. No one to help you when you're down."

"Well, then they should feel sorry for him," I argued.

Auntie shook her head. "But it comes back to one principle: Anything bad that happens to you in this life—and that includes being poor—must be a punishment for something wicked you did in a previous life. Look at him. That's why he's ashamed."

Kong hadn't understood our exchange, but he tried to answer what Auntie had said in Chinese. *"We've managed."* He paused uncomfortably and added, *"At least I thought we had until now. Please. I know I can get Lung to give himself up."*

Auntie looked at me. It was a strange sight to see Kong beg. Poor as he might be, he didn't seem like someone who was used to it. That convinced me. *"Okay. Give him chance,"* I said.

"All right," Auntie said.

Kong looked gratefully at her and then at me. *"You won't regret this,"* he said.

I was already having my doubts; but I didn't say anything as Kong led us back up the steep hill. Auntie hadn't had problems going downhill, but now she started to wheeze after just a few blocks.

Worried, I slowed down to keep pace with her. "It's a good thing you decided to go on a diet."

"I guess," she panted.

Above Grant Avenue the souvenir places stopped and the shops catered to the locals. The groceries stocked anything you needed for a Chinese meal, and the bookstores had the latest magazines from Hong Kong, and the music shops sold the hottest hits from that city. Even the menus taped to the windows of the little restaurants were only in Chinese.

Lung lived in a grimy old brick tenement. The paint on the wooden windowsills had worn off long ago, and the gray wood had weathered smooth as bone.

"He shares an apartment with six old bachelors," Kong said, pointing to a three-story brick building. *"If Lung's there, I'll get him to come out. If he's not, we can wait for him. There's usually someone in the room, and Lung's roommates know me, so they'll let me in. When I get into the room, I'll raise the shade."* He pointed out the window.

I felt a twinge of doubt again, but then Kong said, *"Thank you. You won't regret this."*

I was speechless as he crossed the street. I didn't know the surly street rat knew how to thank anyone.

Maybe Auntie was right. Perhaps he wasn't all bad. As I turned thoughtfully, I caught sight of a bakery with small tables and chairs in the window. "We can wait in there while we watch."

As Kong climbed the steps, Auntie smacked her lips. "All this detecting work makes a woman hungry." Her spirits picked up with each step, and when we entered the doorway, she sniffed the air appreciatively. "Something smells freshly baked."

"Now Auntie, remember your diet," I scolded her.

Auntie looked as if I had just punched her in the stomach. "That's vicious, kiddo. Maybe you should be a lawyer. You know how to go right for the jugular." Even so, when she went to the cashier, she asked only for two teas.

The woman behind the register looked as if she did considerable sampling of the product. "Don't you want to order something else?" she asked. "There's a five-dollar minimum." She pointed to a sign.

"If that's the case . . ." Auntie sidestepped along the glass-fronted counter, studying the contents. There were all sorts of cakes, pies, tarts and other pastries.

"Auntie," I chided her.

"You can eat it," she said, not taking her eyes from the case for one moment. "I'm going to have my dessert vicariously. So I'm going to watch you . . . eat that éclair." She tapped the glass.

I followed Auntie to the window table, sliding into a chair. Auntie gazed mournfully down at the éclair. "Good-bye, little friend."

As I picked up the éclair, I sighed. "The things I do for truth and justice."

Auntie pulled at her tea bag and grumbled, "And all I get to drink is Lipton's." She took a sip. "I hate Lipton's."

I ate my éclair between sips of hot tea while Auntie alternated between watching me and the place across the street.

Suddenly she raised her head. "Is that Kong leaving?"

I looked, but it was only an elderly balding man picking his way down the steps. "It's someone else," I said. From the corner of my eye I caught a movement. Whirling around, I saw Auntie trying to sneak a dollop of cream to her mouth.

"Auntie," I said, examining the gouged-out interior of my éclair, "how could you?"

Auntie's face reddened, and she made a noise in her throat.

I saw that it was time to haul out the big guns. So I invoked the most powerful person in Auntie's life: her agent, Artie. "What will Artie say if you don't get that gig with Clark Tom?"

With bad grace Auntie wiped her finger on a napkin. "I hope you get pimples."

"Auntie!" I sat back, shocked and horrified. I wouldn't wish that curse on my own worst enemy: my brother, Chris.

Auntie realized she had gone too far. "Well," she said, relenting a little, "not big ones."

"I wonder what's taking Kong so long," I muttered. All my old doubts and suspicions quickly came tumbling back.

Auntie shrugged. "Who knows? Perhaps no one was in the room, so he had to wait until one of them came along." She had an answer for every question.

"Why are you always taking his side?" I demanded indignantly.

Auntie sipped from her cup. "Because I know what it's like to have everyone in Chinatown be down on you. When I first decided to go into acting, there was a lot of head shaking and tongue wagging here. Most everyone expected the worst—especially my family. The only one who stuck by me was your grandmother."

I crumbled the Styrofoam lip of the cup. "So you think there's some good in him?"

Auntie nodded. "He's like a beaten dog who's never heard a kind word, only known the stick."

Despite Auntie's faith I was sure Kong and his brother were halfway to Los Angeles by now, but then Auntie pointed excitedly as the shade finally went up in Lung's room. "There's the sign."

Kong appeared in the window and then turned as if he was talking to someone else in the room. Was it Lung? Turning to face the room, he put a hand behind his back and beckoned us to come up.

"Smart boy." Auntie grunted with satisfaction.

I still didn't trust Kong as much as she did. "Maybe it's a trap for us."

Auntie placed her hands on the table. "What have you got against Kong?"

I folded my arms. "He's a snotty little punk."

"And you're behaving just as he would expect a native-born to behave," Auntie said.

"He also lied to us about his brother," I pointed out.

Auntie nodded her head toward the window. "And now he's taking big risks to make up for it."

I stayed glued to my chair. "Or setting us up."

Auntie heaved herself from her chair. "There's only one way to find out, kiddo."

"You're crazy to trust him," I insisted. I was regretting my decision to let him go up there.

Auntie patted me on the arm. "You could be right. You

wait here and call the police if I don't come back in ten minutes."

I couldn't stand on the sidelines while Auntie was charging straight into trouble. "I'm coming along just in case he tries to stab you in the back."

CHAPTER SIXTEEN

We took a staircase to the right that led up two flights. Generations of feet had worn hollows into the wooden steps, and in the dim light that fell through the cracked, dusty windows, I could see that the paint was flaking off the walls, revealing different colors.

Kong leaned over a banister above us. *"There you are,"* he called with forced cheerfulness. *"I've been waiting for you, Auntie."*

He didn't have any right to call her Auntie, and I glared up at him.

"And how are you, Cousin?" he called down to me.

"Play along," Auntie whispered to me.

"Fine," I shouted up to him.

When we reached Kong's landing, Auntie paused to get back her breath. It was hard, though, because the hallway smelled of disinfectant, like a hospital.

Kong put a hand on her arm. *"Are you all right?"*

"I could use a glass of water," Auntie finally said.

"I wouldn't recommend it. The water comes out of the tap

brown with rust. In fact it's more like sludge than liquid," an elderly man said in Chinese from the doorway. He was wearing gray pants and a white shirt.

"Home, sweet home," Auntie said. "It must be hard to wash your clothes."

The man squinted at her. "Do I know you?"

"I've made some movies," Auntie said modestly.

The man raised one hand to point at her. "You were in Feet of Fury."

It was a pleasure meeting someone who knew more about Auntie's career than I did. "You like movie?"

The man nodded his head enthusiastically. "Sure. I only get off Monday nights when the restaurant is closed, so I spend the whole day in the movie theaters. I go to any that has a new movie." He turned to scold Kong. "You should have told me your visitor was famous."

If the poor man had to work six nights a week at his age, I really felt sorry for him.

The man sighed. "This generation's so stupid," he said to Auntie. "People call me Ah Luke."

"You don't mind if we come in?" Auntie asked.

"I'd be honored." Smiling broadly, he stepped back to let Auntie enter the apartment.

The room was small. The light in the room came from a single naked bulb dangling from the dirty ceiling. The room smelled of stale sweat and smoke, but Auntie sailed in as if it was filled with expensive perfume.

As I followed her, I whispered in English, "How many did he say live in there?"

Auntie shrugged. "Seven. They really cram into these

129

tenement apartments, but that's the only way they can afford to live."

"I'll never complain about the size of my room again," I said, feeling guilty.

Ah Luke led Auntie over to one of the bunk beds and made her sit down. *"It might be a while before Lung comes home."*

I glanced at Kong, who was closing the door. He was good at lying. Too good.

"You don't mind?" Auntie asked politely.

"No. I'm going to my job now." He took a black bow tie from his pocket. *"That is, if there's still a job to go to. I worked for the father for years in whatever place he owned. It was okay when he ran things. But the son . . ."* He just shook his head.

"The next generation wastes what the old generation sweated to gather," Auntie said. It sounded like some proverb.

"Isn't that the truth?" the man said, clipping the tie to his collar. *"But I've never seen anyone go through money so fast. The son loses money like it's water in the fist."*

"How so?" Auntie asked.

"How else? Gambling." Ah Luke took a jacket from a bed and put it on. *"The restaurant is sure to go under soon. Sometimes I get so disgusted, I'm ready to quit."*

"You earned your rest," I said.

Ah Luke shrugged one arm into his jacket. *"I tried to retire ten years ago. But what was I supposed to do? Sit around Portsmouth Square? That's for pigeons and the elderly."* It was clear that he didn't include himself in either group.

"Don't you have some family you could live with?" Auntie asked.

Ah Luke slid his arm through the other sleeve. "Oh, sure. I got a boy. But he lives up in Marin. In Corte Madera. And I don't get along with his wife so good. I tried it once, but I came back." He pulled his jacket up around his shoulders and walked out.

As soon as the door shut, Kong started to dig through one pile. "Lung used to keep it in a box." He pulled out an old box and opened it. He breathed a sigh of relief as he held up a tattered paper book. "It's here. At least we know Lung hasn't run away."

Kong thumbed through the book. "It has all of our father's wisdom in it. Proverbs. Quotes from poems and lectures. Also prices so we'd never overpay." He put it back carefully into the box. "It was all he had to leave us."

I began to feel ashamed. Some of us are born with a good hand of cards, and some of us aren't. It didn't seem fair.

As Kong set the box down reverently, I rubbed my nose. "Something smell funny." It took me a moment to identify it. I'd gotten a whiff of it just this afternoon. "Is gunpowder?" I asked. I sat down on the floor.

Puzzled, Kong opened the lid of another box. It was stuffed with red packs of firecrackers. "That was someone else's assignment in the Powell Street Boys. His job was to steal cars."

"He must've stolen some of Errol's stock," Auntie said.

So Lung had access to gunpowder. Had he rigged the tray?

Suddenly I felt vibrations. I heard quick, heavy footsteps. Springing to my feet, I was starting for the door when it opened.

Lung paused in mid step. His mouth tightened when he saw Auntie and me, and then his eyes fastened on Kong. "Traitor!" he said angrily. "You turned me in."

When Kong crouched, ready to fight, I realized he was on our side after all.

Kong pointed his index finger accusingly at Lung. "You're the traitor. Where's your sense of honor? Did you ever stop to think what people would say about me?"

"I can't fight you," Lung said, "so step aside."

Kong stayed glued where he was. "What did you do with the money?"

Lung looked at him as if he was crazy. "What money?"

"This afternoon you stole money and left a bomb in its place," Kong accused him.

Lung spread his arms. "I don't know what you're talking about."

"Why did you steal the flowers from the Wok Inn, and why did you run away from the florist's?" Auntie asked.

"I don't owe you any answers." Lung waved an arm, motioning for his brother to move aside. "I have to leave town."

When Lung stepped toward him, Kong launched himself like a missile. He was a very impressive sight as he flew through the air feet first—until Lung sidestepped. Lung shoved Kong with his hands while he was in midair so that he crashed into a bunk bed. Boxes came cascading down in an avalanche of cardboard.

"Kong," Auntie said, springing to her feet.

"He only trying help you," I yelled at Lung.

Lung straightened up. *"Is he all right?"* he asked.

I shoved boxes out of the way until I saw Kong. His eyes were closed, but he was breathing. *"Yes. No thanks you."*

"When he wakes up, tell him to go back to his master," Lung said. *"He needs more lessons."*

As he started to turn, Auntie hit him with her purse. There was a sharp clonk, and Lung sagged to the floor to join his brother.

"What have you got in your purse? An anvil?" I asked Auntie.

She hefted it in both hands. "Ann asked me to get rolls of coins to make change. I forgot they were in here. No wonder I've been huffing and puffing."

CHAPTER SEVENTEEN

Kong was the first to wake up. *"Where am I?"* he asked, sitting up groggily. Auntie and I were sitting on top of Lung.

"In your brother's room," she said.

Kong scowled as his memory came back to him. *"That dog,"* he said, glaring at his brother.

"Insult while help us sit on him," I said, waving him over.

"Why don't you just tie him up?" he asked, rubbing the bump on his head.

"No rope," I said.

"You don't need rope. We've got his clothes." He found Lung's shirts and T-shirts and pants among the boxes and began twisting and tying them into a rope.

With Kong's help we tied up his brother. When we were finished, I asked him, *"Is telephone? We should call police."*

He nodded toward the hallway. *"There's a pay telephone outside, but don't phone them just yet. Let me talk to Lung."*

"He attacked you," Auntie pointed out.

He frowned at his brother. *"I need to know why."* He walked out and came back a moment later with a glass of water. He splashed some of it over Lung.

Lung woke spluttering and angry. He used some choice words in Chinese and then spat at Kong. Kong calmly poured the rest of the water over his brother.

"You can drown," Kong explained, *"or you can answer our questions."*

Lung's only response was to wriggle like a worm on the floor, trying to break his bonds. Kong placed his foot on Lung's stomach. *"Where do you want me to start kicking?"*

Lung frowned at his brother but lay still. *"Why did you tell them about me?"*

"Why did you try to kill us with the van?" Kong shot back.

Lung tried to sit up in surprise. *"What are you talking about? Do you really think I could do something like that?"*

"Liar," Kong said, using his foot to pin his brother to the floor. They struggled for a moment before Auntie put a hand on Kong's arm to make him let go.

"Lung, where were you before you came here?" she asked.

I think Lung would have bitten her if she had been close enough. As it was, all he could do was sit up. *"None of your business."*

"Answer her," Kong warned, *"or she'll hit you with her purse again."*

Lung looked at Auntie's purse with new respect. *"They should make you get a license for that weapon."*

I knelt down so I could make eye contact. *"Please. It important."*

He studied me for a moment, and he must have decided I was harmless. "*I was collecting some money I had lent a friend. So I could get away.*"

Auntie and I exchanged glances. Whoever had stolen the lettuce money wouldn't have needed to borrow money. Kong realized that too.

"*Then you didn't steal the lettuce money or the van?*" he asked.

"*No!*" Lung snapped.

"*If he not drive van, who did? Who stole lettuce money?*" I asked Auntie.

Auntie shook her head. She asked Lung, "*Why did you try to steal the carnations?*"

"*I was told to,*" Lung said, bracing himself against a bed.

"*By whom?*" Auntie asked.

"*The same person who told me to swap the white carnations for the original floral arrangement.*" Lung wriggled his nose. "*I got an itch.*"

Auntie carefully extended an index finger, ready to pull it back just in case Lung decided to bite. When he didn't, she gently scratched the tip of his nose with a manicured, scarlet-red fingernail. I recognized Mom's painstaking work on Auntie's hands.

"*Who told you to change the order?*" she asked.

Lung sighed in relief now that his itch had been satisfied. "*I don't know. Some man. He only spoke to me on the telephone.*"

"*Did you write the extortion notes too?*" Auntie asked.

He squirmed around on the floor so he could rest

his back against a bunk bed. "Yes, *but he dictated them to me.*"

"*You dog.*" Kong scowled.

"*I quit the gang,*" Lung snapped, thumping his heels for emphasis. "*I was trying to go straight. I'd taken the job at the florist's to save enough so I could start over in Los Angeles.*"

Kong squatted and touched his brother's leg. "*Why didn't you tell me you'd quit the gang?*"

"*The last time we saw one another, we fought,*" Lung growled.

"*Do you think gang track you down and call you?*" I asked.

Lung shook his head. "*I would have recognized the voice if it was someone in the Powell Street Boys. But I wouldn't put it past the gang to sell the information to someone else. The blackmailer knew names, dates—stuff that I had done for the gang. He said he'd pass on all the info to the police if I didn't do exactly what he said.*"

Kong wasn't about to cut his brother any slack. "*Or maybe you're lying about the voice. Maybe you just got impatient because you couldn't save enough money fast enough. So you thought you'd use one of the Powell Street Boys' schemes and extort the money from the restaurant. And when they ignored you, you decided just to take the money yourself.*"

"*What do you know about patience?*" Lung demanded indignantly. "*You live with that martial arts dinosaur, and you get to eat all you want.*"

I thought Kong was going to hit Lung, so I held his arm. "*Easy. Maybe he tell truth.*"

Kong shook free. "*He's forgotten what the truth is.*"

I appealed to Auntie. "*We not call police yet, until we figure out if Lung tell truth or not.*"

"*The extortion notes involve Ann and Morgan,*" Auntie said. "*They have to decide.*"

"*Did the notes upset them?*" Lung asked guiltily.

I remembered the scene after the explosion. "*How you feel if you got them and then bomb go off?*"

Lung was totally bewildered. "*You mentioned a bomb before. What bomb?*"

So we told him what had gone on—from the lion dance to the van. When we were finished, he swore, "*I didn't take any money or set any bomb. I just sent the notes and flowers. I left the restaurant right after I dropped off the flowers. I didn't go back there until I got the call to steal them back. You can check with Mr. Errol. I was making deliveries. And I didn't have time to steal a van and try to run you over.*"

Auntie rubbed her hands together unhappily. "*Extortion is a serious business. You have to let your victims decide.*"

"*Untie me, and I'll go with you to the restaurant,*" Lung said.

"*They're at Wesleyan,*" Auntie said, and nodded to me. "*We should go there anyway, to see how Barry and Scott are doing.*"

"*Is that near Chinatown?*" Kong asked nervously.

Auntie turned one way and then another, trying to fix the direction, and wound up waving her hand vaguely toward the south. "*It's over in the Mission District.*"

"*So far?*" Kong asked. He made it sound like we had asked him to accompany us to Iceland.

I thought he was afraid of that area. *"It in safe neighborhood,"* I said.

Lung swallowed. *"Leave Chinatown?"*

At first I thought the brothers were trying to weasel out of their promise. *"You give word,"* I said angrily.

"But so far," Kong repeated.

My temper had finally reached the boiling point. He thought he was so superior to "hollow bamboo," when he was the one who was trapped. I wanted to tell him that and a lot more, but it was beyond my fractured Chinese.

It made me feel so . . . so frustrated, even illiterate. Then I realized that this must be the way Kong felt with English.

So what if things were reversed? What if we were in Hong Kong? I'd probably skip school as much as I could, because my Chinese wouldn't be good enough to understand the teachers. With my broken Chinese, I would only be able to get a lousy, low-paying job. In short, I'd be trapped, with no way out.

I began to feel sorry for him. The few blocks to his master's studio were as far as Kong wanted to travel.

The brothers looked at one another, and then Lung shook his head. *"We'd rather stay here."*

"You must have left Chinatown when you made your deliveries," Auntie said to Lung.

Lung shrugged. *"Most of Mr. Errol's deliveries were in Chinatown. And the few that weren't . . . well, the first couple of times I would just go to the Square and have a few smokes. Then I'd go back and tell Mr. Errol that I'd got lost. Eventually he gave up asking and did them himself."*

"*I surprised you not get fired,*" I said.

"*Who else would he find to work for three dollars an hour?*" Lung said.

Auntie rubbed her chin with her thumb. "*I think you really should come with us.*"

"*If we wanted to run away, you couldn't stop us,*" Kong said. "*But if you set a time and a place, we'll meet you.*"

"*On our honor,*" Lung added, and Kong nodded.

I wasn't sure that was good enough, and Auntie herself hesitated.

I said, "*Give your father's journal. We give back you when we see you.*"

Lung butted his brother's arm with his head. "*You told them?*"

Kong, though, ignored him. "*Take it.*"

"*But Father's journal,*" Lung protested.

"*You can trust them. They're not bad for native-born,*" he replied.

That was as close to a compliment as I had heard from Kong. "*Why you change mind about 'hollow bamboo'?*" I asked in surprise.

Kong scratched his head sheepishly. "*I've spent time with you now. I never got to do that before.*"

"*What your master say?*" I teased.

"*I'm beginning to think he doesn't know everything,*" Kong said.

"*Maybe you're growing up after all, little brother,*" Lung said.

"*Maybe you are too.*" Kong shrugged, and he began to untie his brother.

Lifting the journal carefully from its box, Auntie stowed it in her purse.

"*We'll meet at the Square in two hours. Okay?*" she asked.

"*We'll be there,*" Kong promised.

"*And bring back the journal,*" Lung warned darkly, "*or else.*"

CHAPTER EIGHTEEN

So we headed over to the bus stop to catch a bus to Wesleyan Hospital.

We had barely squeezed onto the bottom step of the bus when the driver shut the doors. I managed to thrust an arm through a tangle of limbs and torsos and found a railing to hold on to. "Hold on to me," I said to Auntie.

Though Auntie looked a little dazed, she took my shoulder while the bus lurched and grumbled its way down the street. I was used to the warfare that they call the San Francisco Muni. I suppose in most cities being a passenger is a passive pastime, but in mine it's a job. Auntie wasn't used to this anymore, so I had to watch out for her.

Telling Auntie to follow me, I worked our way up the steps and into the bus itself—past sharp elbows, over bursting plastic shopping bags and dodging backpacks that swayed like camel humps.

A young Afro-American woman in a skirt and suit coat got up. "Ma'am," she said to Auntie, "would you like my seat?"

Instantly, a Chinese girl with long black hair slid into the vacated seat, and she began chatting away in Chinese with another girl. But they spoke too fast for me to follow.

"That seat was meant for this poor old lady," the Afro-American woman scolded her.

Auntie recovered enough of her dignity to shake her head. "I'm not that old."

However, the Afro-American woman was too busy poking the girl in the shoulder to pay attention to Auntie. "Hey, get out of that chair. If she doesn't want it, I want it back."

"You left," the girl said sullenly.

The argument went on all the way to Market Street, the main thoroughfare that cuts diagonally across the heart of San Francisco. As we stumbled off the bus, Auntie tried to pat her hair back into some semblance of its usual shape. "After this I think I'll hitchhike."

Market Street wasn't like the old photos Auntie had once shown me. Back when Auntie was my age— when women and girls wore white cotton gloves to shop— downtown had been a pleasant place where most people came to buy stuff. Since then, most of the department stores had fled for the suburbs, and those that were left were slowly falling apart. There was a fortress mentality everywhere. There were bars and steel doors and curtains to protect most shops.

"San Francisco's changed so much, kiddo." Auntie sighed.

Wesleyan Hospital was an odd pile of bricks that looked like two or three buildings joined together.

Inside, Auntie headed over to the information desk. A large woman sat behind the desk watching television. On her sweater was a plastic badge that said VOLUNTEER.

"We're looking for Barry Fisher," Auntie said.

Reluctantly the volunteer took her eyes from the television and turned to a monitor in front of her. Her fingers clicked across the keys. "Room five-oh-one."

"Five-oh-one," Auntie repeated, and she took a step away, then hesitated. "And where are the elevators?"

The volunteer had returned to her soap opera. Without taking her eyes from the screen, she pointed toward the floor. "Follow the yellow line."

When we arrived on the fifth floor, we followed the signs that led us to 501, all the way down at the end of a hallway. Barry lay in bed with the upper half of his face wrapped tightly in bandages.

Ann sat in an orange plastic chair holding on to his hand, while Morgan and Uncle Leonard sat near her. She leaped up when she saw us. "Oh, Auntie." Though we were no blood kin, almost everyone called Auntie by that title. Auntie patted Ann on the back. "There, there, kiddo. How are the boys?"

Morgan was extending his hand even before he stood up. "The doctor says that Barry's blindness is only temporary. Scott's only got a sprain, so he went home."

Auntie shook hands with him. I was glad to hear about Scott but worried about Barry. "I'll bring you your homework," I told Barry, "and I'll help read it to you."

Barry nodded gratefully.

Auntie said some encouraging things to Barry and

then turned to Ann. "We think we found the boy who delivered the extortion notes to you, but not who stole the money."

"This time we're going to the police," Morgan said.

"Whoa," Auntie said. "We just found the messenger, not the mastermind." And she told Ann and Morgan about everything we had done. "So we thought we'd leave it up to you."

"What do you think, Barry?" Ann asked her son. "If this boy helps us locate the extortionist, should we ask the police to take it easy on him?"

Barry's hand groped across the bed until it found Ann's and gave it a hard squeeze.

"The boy will also have to testify," Morgan said.

"If it was a question of squaring things with you, I guess he would," Auntie said. I wasn't sure Lung would agree to that.

"But who stole the money then?" Morgan asked.

Uncle Leonard got up abruptly from his chair. "I'd stay if I could, but I've got a meeting."

"We'll manage," Ann said.

As Uncle Leonard lifted his coat from the back of his chair, still carrying his pink box, something fluttered from his pocket.

"Wait," I said as he hurried from the room.

"Can't," he called over his shoulder.

I bent to pick up the object he had dropped. It was a folded-up green rectangle of paper. My eyes widened when I saw the 100 in numerals. "How much cash does he carry around?"

Ann smiled with one corner of her mouth. "My brother always likes to flash a big roll of money. It made it easy to buy his Christmas presents. We used to just give him money clips."

"You can return it to him," I said, starting to hand it to her.

Auntie's hand intercepted it. "I'd like to see that hundred-dollar bill," she said.

"You don't think . . ." Ann closed her mouth quickly, horrified.

Auntie opened her purse. "When I picked up the hundred-dollar bills for you"—she took out a sheet of paper that had been folded in thirds—"the bank also gave me a list of the serial numbers. I forgot to give it to you when I handed over the money."

"Leonard's capable of being mean and petty, but he wouldn't swipe the money like a common thief," Morgan objected.

"Let's see." Unfolding her list on a table, Auntie checked the bill.

Then her finger ran down the column. I was surprised when her finger stopped and jabbed a number. "Bingo."

"I can't believe it," Ann said.

"You check then." Auntie slid the sheet over so Ann could compare the number to the list. They must have matched; Ann started to shake her head. "I never thought he'd take the feud this far, to steal from his family and to hurt his own nephews."

Ann plopped down onto a chair. "You know how

Chinatown feuds are. They're the worst between blood relatives."

"The explosion might have been an accident," Auntie replied. "He wanted to cover up the theft by destroying the evidence—only he overestimated the explosives. He's an amateur, after all. I don't think he meant to hurt the boys."

"I don't know how long Leonard was in the kitchen before I noticed him. He probably had plenty of time to replace the hundred-dollar bills with the singles," I said.

"May I?" Morgan asked. Anger and disbelief warred in his face as he compared the serial number to the list. "That scum."

Ann's shoulders sagged. "He must have figured how thin I'm stretched. First he tried the extortion notes, then the bomb. And he knew I'd have to make up the losses— with money that I don't have. He must really hate me."

We could hear nurses walking by outside in their squeaky shoes. Gurneys and wheelchairs rattled by, but inside Barry's room the five of us were silent. Since Auntie had set up her public relations business, we had met some ugly characters. I liked to believe that there was some good in every person, and that was true. However, it was also true that there was some bad in quite a few people.

I guessed Uncle Leonard was one of those.

CHAPTER NINETEEN

Morgan started to reach for the phone. "I'll call the police."

Suddenly Barry spoke up from the bed. "Let's see if he has any other bills first," he said. "There might be a reasonable explanation for this. Uncle Leonard deserves that much at least. Please."

Morgan took his hand. "This is something the police should handle, son. I wondered what he had in that pink box of his that he wouldn't let go of—I wouldn't either if it was two thousand dollars."

"And what if Uncle Leonard wasn't the thief?" Barry said loyally. "What if there's some other explanation for the hundred-dollar bill? His reputation could be ruined if word got out that he was being investigated."

Ann reluctantly agreed. "Barry is right. That would kill my mother too. I mean, maybe the hundred-dollar bill fell on the floor when the thief—whoever it is—stole it. And he found it and tucked it into his pocket. We have to be fair."

"Tiger Lil, everyone in Chinatown talks about how clever you are. Couldn't you find a way to peek inside the box?" Barry asked.

Thoughtfully, Auntie put the list back into her purse and snapped it shut. "Maybe."

We stayed with them a little longer, but once we were back in the corridor, Auntie put her hands on both my shoulders. "It's time for you to go home, kiddo."

Auntie was such a good actor that sometimes it was hard to tell when she really felt confident and when she was pretending. However, I wasn't buying any of it. "While the villains are chasing you around the room, you'll need someone to dial nine-one-one," I said stubbornly.

Auntie studied me. "How come your mom and dad are so levelheaded, and you're not?"

I could give back as good as I got. "They say it skips a generation."

Auntie chuckled. Despite everything, she seemed pleased. "They didn't name you Lily for nothing."

We decided the most likely place to find Uncle Leonard and his pink box was at his restaurant, Ciao Chow, which lay in the heart of the financial district. Like a high-tech tidal wave, the district's tall skyscrapers of steel and glass towered over the small buildings of Chinatown to the west.

Auntie had once helped a client give a party at Ciao Chow, which was how she had met Ann and Morgan when they still worked there. I could see, through the big plate-glass windows, that Uncle Leonard had put it through another facelift since I had been there last. He'd gone for a chrome look with basic black and white squares. Even the waitpersons had checkered jackets, and on their heads were little hats like the tops of chess pieces. Behind the cash register was a woman in a checkered dress with a chess queen's cap on her head.

There seemed to be more staff than customers inside. When Ann and Morgan had run the place, it had been packed. Maybe the head of lettuce had been too tempting for Uncle Leonard. I mentioned that to Auntie.

"He might even have considered it his due," Auntie agreed. "Compensation for loss of customers when they left."

"Would he really carry his grudge that far?" I asked.

Auntie chuckled. "Most Chinese Americans come from southern China. In China, that region has a reputation for feuds."

"But we're in America," I said.

"It's in the genes," Auntie said, "but most of us keep it under control."

An elderly Chinese man in gray pants and a white shirt was cleaning the sidewalk with a bucket of soapy water and a broom. He glanced up at us as we passed around him, careful to stay on the dry area as we headed for the lobby door.

"If you had asked me, I would have recommended some better places to eat," the man said to Auntie.

It was Ah Luke who had been doing the sidewalk.

Auntie pivoted in surprise. *"I didn't know you worked here."*

"I've worked at each of the family's restaurants," Ah Luke

said, leaning his broom against the window. *"The boss said I was his good luck charm. And when he died, the boss's wife asked me to stick around and help her children. When they sold the old place and opened this one, I had my doubts, but the daughter knew what she was doing."*

"I gave a party here one evening," Auntie said. *"I'm surprised I didn't meet you back then."*

"I must have been in back," Ah Luke said. Picking up the bucket, he headed toward the curb. *"The food's been rotten ever since Miss Ann left. I wanted to help them both, but what could I do? I couldn't split myself in two."* He sounded guilty. *"Since Leonard took over, this place has been going downhill."*

Auntie tried to sound casual when she asked, *"Is Leonard inside?"*

Ah Luke threw the soapy water into the gutter with a loud splash. *"That one? He came for a few minutes and then left. I suppose he's off gambling. I don't see why he just doesn't hand the money over to those people and be done with it."*

"Was he . . . was he carrying a pink box?" Auntie pantomimed holding a box by its ribbon.

Ah Luke turned the bucket upside down and drummed its bottom to get out the last few drops. *"Yes. I thought it was funny, but I figured he was trying to get his gambling friends into a good mood by bringing them treats."*

"Luke," the cashier said from the lobby doorway, "stop talking. Get back in here."

I was surprised when Ah Luke just stayed where he was.

"If you don't get back in here this instant, you're fired."
Furious, the cashier headed toward us. Almost immediately
she threw up her arms for balance. In her hurry, she had
charged onto the part of the sidewalk that was still slick
with soap suds. Her feet went out from under her, and she
was sliding across the pavement.

Ah Luke ignored her, heading back toward the window
instead, the bucket banging against his leg.

"Are you okay?" I asked, going over to the cashier
as she lay on the damp concrete.

Even though she clung to me to help her to her feet,
she was glaring at Ah Luke. "That does it. You're fired.
Don't bother coming back."

With a smile, Ah Luke pantomimed putting a telephone receiver to his ear and pretended to dial.

The cashier's mouth opened and then clamped shut.
In her stocking feet, she whirled around and headed
back to the restaurant. The entire back of her dress was
wet.

Ah Luke leisurely picked up one of her shoes and
held out his hand toward me. *Fetch the other shoe, will
you?*

The shoe lay about three yards away. When I had
snagged it and handed it to him, he pitched both of them
into the lobby underhand as if they were horseshoes. The
cashier reappeared momentarily. She picked them up,
glared at us murderously and then retreated to the shelter
of her cash register.

Astounded, Auntie was already digging out one
of her business cards to give Ah Luke, as she had done for

Bernie. "I'm sorry we got you fired. But here—give me a call, and maybe I can help."

Ah Luke took the card reverently, holding it by the edges between his fingertips. *"Thank you for the souvenir,"* he said, and then he held it out shyly toward Auntie. *"Would you sign it?"*

Auntie dug a pen from her purse and used the purse to lean on. *"I really mean it. Call me."*

Ah Luke took the card back and studied the autograph before he held it out toward Auntie again. *"In Chinese, please."*

Ah Luke definitely had his own way of doing things— whether it was being fired or getting an autograph.

"Certainly," Auntie said. She got out her pen again and signed her Chinese name. *"Please call me."*

Ah Luke studied the Chinese characters critically. *"Spring Lily. Is that your real name or your screen name?"*

Auntie capped her pen and restored it to her purse. *"Both. Don't be afraid to phone,"* she urged him again.

Ah Luke put the card carefully into a worn old billfold and stuffed it into his back pocket. *"Thank you. But you really don't have to worry about me."*

I was so surprised that I resorted to Chinese, though Kong had made me feel self-conscious. *"But you fired."*

Ah Luke went over to a faucet in the wall and turned the brass knob. *"They try to fire me every week. In fact they've been trying to fire me for six years. I just go on with my job."*

I looked at Auntie for help with the conversation, but for once she was at a loss for words too. With a smile,

Ah Luke went over and picked up a hose that lay there. *"They know if they get me upset, I'll call the real boss. Leonard owns this place, but his mother's the actual boss."*

Auntie lifted her head as she understood. "Ann and Leonard's mother." That's why Ah Luke's little pantomime had shut the cashier up.

Ah Luke squeezed the trigger on the hose nozzle, and a white jet of water slammed against the sidewalk. *"You're not here to eat, are you?"*

Auntie used all her acting skill to appear innocent. *"What makes you think that?"*

Ah Luke went about methodically cleaning the sidewalk with controlled blasts, using the water as skillfully as if it was a broad broom. *"Because no one comes here to eat anymore except tourists who don't know any better."*

"No, *we're* not," Auntie admitted, and she told him about our suspicions that Uncle Leonard had stolen money from Ann.

The water jet sprayed back and forth as he shook his head in dismay. *"That fool. I knew he'd get deeper into trouble. He'll lose his mother's restaurant and everything else."*

Uncle Leonard might hold the title of manager, but Ah Luke seemed to consider the restaurant his own, in spirit if not in fact.

"Deeper into what kind of trouble?" Auntie asked sharply.

"That one likes to throw his money away at Coyote's. He's always needing money. The bookkeeper complains that she has to cook the books all the time to hide the money he skims right

out of the till." Ah Luke let go of the trigger, and the water spray stopped.

Auntie snapped her fingers. "*Isn't Coyote's that new southwestern place?*"

He went over to the faucet and shut it off. "*I don't know what kind it is. It's one of those places that changes every week to match a new trend. The only thing that remains the same is the poker game in a back room. I have a friend who washes dishes there.*"

Ah Luke unscrewed the hose from the faucet. "*He must really be desperate if he's stealing from his sister now.*"

"*And he may have put his two nephews into the hospital too,*" I said.

He sighed with tragic sorrow. "*The family's come to this.*"

Auntie began to look around the street. "*We'd better find a telephone book and look up Coyote's.*"

Ah Luke began to coil up the hose, which slithered toward him with each loop. "*I can tell you the address. I bring Leonard's payments over there to settle his debts.*"

"*Can I have it?*" Auntie asked.

Ah Luke heaved the coiled green hose up his arm and onto his shoulder. "*First you have to promise to tell me what you find out.*"

Auntie was suddenly wary. "*Why?*"

He picked up the bucket and squeegee. "*I owe it to the boss's wife to try to warn her about any danger to her family's reputation,*" he said. There was only one boss to Ah Luke, and that certainly did not include Uncle Leonard. "*I don't care what you do to the son.*"

"*You have my word,*" Auntie said.

Ah Luke took the top from the faucet—I guess so no prankster would be able to turn it on. "*It's over on Fillmore,*" he said, and he gave her the address.

Auntie started to look around. "*That's over in Pacific Heights. We'd better get a cab.*"

I started to hail a cab, but Auntie put her hand on my arm and forced me to lower it. "We need to find a Chinese bakery or deli first."

I frowned. It was hard trying to be Auntie's conscience when she was on a diet. "This is no time for snacking."

"For a pink box, kiddo. They're generic all over Chinatown," Auntie said. "With a little luck we can pull the old switcheroo."

As she started to walk briskly in search of a bakery, I trotted along. "You're awfully good at tricks. Just what sort of crowd did you hang out with in Hollywood?"

"Only with saints and angels, kiddo," Auntie said, puffing. She still had Ann's change in her purse. "Haven't you read my old bios from the studios?"

The first bakery we tried had already closed, and though we could see an aproned clerk inside, he was busy mopping up. When Auntie banged on the window, he just shook his head and went on cleaning up.

The next couple of places were shut up just as tightly.

Our quest for a box brought us back to the bakery where we had waited while Kong went to find Lung.

The clerk looked up when we entered. "Five dollar—" she began to say as she pointed at a sign.

"We know," Auntie said, putting on her most winning

smile. "All I want is a box." She pointed to a stack of empty boxes that were identical to the one Leonard had.

The clerk looked around for a sign to point to, but for once she'd come across a situation for which she didn't have a sign. "Boxes are for our wares," she finally explained.

"But I just need a box," Auntie coaxed.

"Can't sell a box without my wares inside it," the clerk said, folding her arms.

Auntie tried her best, but she couldn't budge the clerk. "All right," she finally sighed. "Give me a cake."

"Auntie," I said sternly.

"This is for Ann," Auntie rationalized. "We need something to weigh the box down anyway."

"Which cake do you want?" the clerk asked.

Auntie took out a twenty-dollar bill as she studied the counter. Her eyes drifted over the top shelf and then the bottom shelf as if she was mentally devouring everything inside. She wound up fastening onto a small chocolate cake. "That one," she said, tapping her finger against the counter.

Auntie paid for the cake with her twenty-dollar bill. When the clerk tied string around the box, she squinted. "Weren't you in here before?"

"We just loved the service here," Auntie said.

The clerk tipped her head back, looking as if she was trying to decide if Auntie was telling the truth or being sarcastic.

"Come on," I said, picking up the box. "We've lost enough time."

As Auntie and I shoved the door open, I could see the clerk from the corner of my eye. She had her pen out and was busy scribbling something on a sheet of paper. I was sure it was a sign informing the buying public that boxes were only for her wares.

CHAPTER TWENTY

Once outside, I started to wave my arms without much luck. Then Auntie put two fingers into her mouth and let out a deafening whistle.

I hadn't noticed the cab before, because it was in the middle of traffic. Cars honked as the cabby swung his taxi recklessly through traffic and over to the curb.

He knew where Coyote's was, and he took us out to Fillmore as soon as Auntie asked. Back when San Francisco was just starting out, people had called it Cow Hollow. Now it had turned into an area where the yuppies lived. It was full of trendy clothing stores, bars and restaurants, and the sidewalks were crowded with young, well-dressed people. The fog was drifting in from the ocean, putting them into even more of a rush to get inside to the warmth of various places.

Soon enough I saw the huge neon sign in the shape of a cactus. Flashing red letters announced that we were at Coyote's. Auntie paid the cabby, giving him a fifty-cent tip, which didn't exactly please him.

On the outside, the place looked like it was made of adobe bricks. When I poked one, though, I realized it was only plaster painted to look like adobe.

I hunted for Uncle Leonard inside but didn't see him. "I think we've got to go in."

Auntie shuddered after she checked out the prices on the menu. "All we can afford to drink is water, kiddo," she said as we went in.

The interior had a western motif with wagon wheels and coyotes with bandannas tied around their necks. Everything looked as if it had come straight out of a cartoon. Big plaster cacti sprouted from the floor. Tinier cacti in painted pots sat on each table. Next to each miniature cactus was a candle in a red glass holder shaped like an upside-down cowboy hat.

"I bet the interior decorator has never been east of the bay," Auntie muttered to me.

Suddenly I saw Uncle Leonard's head floating above the rest of the crowd in the bar. "There he is," I said.

A hostess in a white gown slit up the side came over toward us. Her hair had been braided and then piled up on her head, and I would have said she easily had a hundred dollars' worth of cosmetics slapped onto her face. There was a huge sheriff's star pinned near her collar. "How many?"

"Two," Auntie said as she took a matchbook from a little cup.

The hostess picked up two huge menus from behind her lectern. "This way," she said.

However, Uncle Leonard sat on a stool at the bar, so

I pointed at a table that would let us keep an eye on him. "How about that one?"

The hostess shrugged as if she couldn't care less. Pulling out a chair, she turned to Auntie. "Madame?"

Auntie was lingering by the dessert tray. She pointed to an especially puffy and gooey chocolate dish. "What's this?"

"Chocolate sin," the hostess said, and she added mischievously, "Perhaps madame would like to start with dessert first?"

I went over and snagged Auntie's arm. "Remember why we're here," I said in a low voice.

Reluctantly Auntie tore her eyes away from the tray and let me guide her to the table. The hostess waited patiently until she could help Auntie to sit down. I plopped down in a chair opposite her.

When Auntie set the cake box on the table, the hostess teased, "We have a wonderful selection of desserts, madame. You didn't have to bring your own."

"I know." Auntie caressed the top of the box. "This is for later, when we get home. My great-niece will get hungry later. You know what a big appetite growing girls have."

"Hey," I said indignantly.

"You're going to be more than full after we're done with you. Well, Debby will be your waitron for the evening," the hostess informed us, and with a breezy "Enjoy," she left us for the next couple waiting by the entrance.

Outside the big windows, the fog floated by like ghostly ribbons. It made me glad to be inside where it was warm.

The menus were bigger than the tiny tabletop, so it took some maneuvering as we both spread them open. "If it isn't Cajun blackened, it's mesquite grilled," Auntie grumbled.

"What's lamb's surprise?" I asked.

"Even if we could afford it—which we can't—you wouldn't like that," Auntie said.

"How do you know?" I asked.

Auntie rattled her menu. "Because it's a euphemism for testicles."

I was just closing my menu when Debby the waitron came over. She was a perky young woman in a ten-gallon hat and a vest. Setting down a bowl of bread, she pulled an order pad from her gun belt. "Would you like something to drink before dinner?"

"No, we're still trying to pick out something. Everything looks so delicious," Auntie said, hiding her nose in her menu.

"We have some lovely specials. First we have salmon in parchment. Cooked with fresh cilantro and capers." I waited for Auntie to cut her off, but I suppose she was enjoying this. At each dish she looked hungrier and hungrier, until Debby ran out of specials.

"We need more time to choose," Auntie said with the self-control of a saint.

"But save room for dessert," Debby urged.

Then Auntie eyed Debby professionally. "You're very good. Are you an actor?"

Debby was startled. "Why, yes. How could you tell?"

"Because no one else would sound so convincing when

they told me I needed another inch of blubber." Auntie turned a page in her menu. "Who represents you?"

"No one at the moment," Debby confessed. "I just graduated from State."

Auntie leaned her elbows on the table. "What else do you do? Sing? Dance?"

"Auntie," I whispered, and I nodded toward the bar to remind her why we were there in the first place. This was no time to be auditioning clients.

Auntie took out her card. "Call this number. I have a friend who is an agent who can help you."

Debby took it and put it carefully inside her suit pocket. "Thank you."

I'd been keeping one eye on Leonard. When his drink arrived, he set the box beneath his feet. I nodded to Auntie. "I think it's time for the old switcheroo."

"What's that?" Debby asked, puzzled.

"My great-niece is from Australia," Auntie ad libbed. "It's what they call a rest room down there."

"Yes." She pointed to the back of the dining area. "You turn left behind the plaster cow."

When Debby had left, Auntie set her menu down and picked up a slice of bread.

"Auntie, remember your diet," I warned her.

"I'm hungry," Auntie complained. "One piece of bread won't hurt."

My own stomach reminded me of how hungry I was, so I took a slice too. However, Auntie wolfed down her slice and started on a second before I had gotten halfway through mine.

"Auntie," I said.

"What?" she asked testily. "I've exercised a lot today."

When she took a third, I grabbed the bowl and set it on the floor by me. "That's enough."

"I was going to stop anyway." She took the matchbook from her coat pocket, sliding the matches over to me. "In five minutes, call the restaurant and ask for Leonard." Picking up the box, she rose before I could stop her.

"Be careful," I warned her.

"Aren't I always?" She winked at me and then made her way around the table.

CHAPTER TWENTY-ONE

I watched as Auntie charged off like a riverboat with a full head of steam. The people around the bar were in their twenties and either very handsome or very pretty. Everyone wore a suit, but the men had their ties loose under their collars. The women wore blouses with big, ugly bows. Above the cow's skull on the wall was a sign that proclaimed: WORK HARD. PLAY HARD. And the crowd there seemed determined to do exactly that.

Auntie navigated her way through the cheerful mob as nimbly as a halfback through a bunch of linebackers. Uncle Leonard sat glumly by himself, nursing a glass of wine as he stared up at the television where a rock video was blaring away.

Careful to keep out of Uncle Leonard's view, Auntie sneaked up behind him and set her own box down on the floor. Then she tapped him on the shoulder. When Uncle Leonard swiveled around, he was unpleasantly surprised to see Auntie.

"One elephant," I murmured to myself. "Two elephants."

With a broad smile Auntie started working on Uncle Leonard. In the noisy restaurant I couldn't hear them, but I could see Auntie's friendly, mobile face chatting on. She would never be at a loss for words. As she spoke, Uncle Leonard seemed to be getting more and more annoyed. He was so busy scowling at Auntie that he didn't notice her foot edging beneath his stool.

I watched breathlessly as slowly, inch by inch, she shoved his box under the next stool. And then, just as carefully, she pushed her cake into the vacated spot under his stool.

"Two hundred and ninety-nine elephants," I counted. "Three hundred elephants." It was time.

Getting up, I moseyed on over to Debby and asked for the pay phones. "By the rest rooms," she said, pointing toward the back. "You hang a left just behind—"

"The cow, thanks," I said. Auntie was still chattering on, and Uncle Leonard was scowling even worse as I got near the huge cow. It was life size, with white spots on its brown hide. People could write messages on the spots with the pen that hung from a string.

I hung a left and went down a hallway. Sure enough, there was a pay telephone on the fake adobe wall just before the rest rooms marked COWGIRLS and COWBOYS. Putting in a quarter, I took out the matchbook and dialed the number. When I heard the hostess's voice, I tried to lower mine so it sounded older. "May I speak to Leonard Lee, please? He should be at the bar."

The hostess didn't ask for a description, which confirmed that Uncle Leonard was a regular. "Just a moment."

I set the receiver on top of the pay telephone and headed out just in time to see Uncle Leonard slide off his high seat. The hostess was already walking back to the front. Auntie bent and reached underneath his stool. "Don't forget your box," she said helpfully.

Awkwardly Uncle Leonard stepped to the side as Auntie hooked her fingers through the strings around the box with the cake. "Give me that," he said nervously.

"No, I've got it." As she pulled out the box we had brought, Auntie was careful to block his view of his own box under the other stool.

"Thank you," Uncle Leonard said. He snatched up the box, cradling it in his arms as if it was as precious as a baby as he went toward the phone.

As he hurried away, Auntie bent down again. "Excuse me," she said to the woman on the stool next to Uncle Leonard's. And she dragged out Uncle Leonard's box.

"Let's go," Auntie whispered.

As I followed her toward the plaster cow, I asked, "If it's not the stolen money, how are you going to get it back to him?"

"Just like we got it in the first place." Auntie glanced down at her hips, which had shielded Uncle Leonard's box from his view. "You know, if I wasn't so big, it wouldn't have been so easy."

It sounded to me like Auntie was angling toward a raid on the dessert tray. "Auntie," I said, exasperated.

"Auntie," she repeated but in an exaggerated whine.

I loved my aunt, but she could be such a pain some-times. There were ten biblical plagues, and Auntie's diet ought to be included with them. "You've been doing real good up to now," I tried to reassure her.

"You're relentless," she snapped. "Do you know that?"

"Clark Tom, Clark Tom," I whispered. "And when the casting directors see you shine on TV, your phone will be ringing off the hook. TV miniseries, cable specials and then the big time, feature films."

"You could have given lessons to the snake in the Garden of Eden," she grumbled as we headed toward the rest rooms.

When we reached the cowgirls' room, she put her hand on the door and opened it cautiously so we could peek inside. The decorator had definitely gotten carried away with cow skulls. They hung everywhere, making it look more like an cow cemetery than a rest room.

The sink sat in a broad slab of red sandstone, and Auntie set the box down on the countertop. "Warn me if anyone's coming, kiddo," she said as she flexed her fingers.

I kept one eye on the door and the other on Auntie. Slipping her fingers beneath the ribbons, she began tugging them gently off the box. When she had one set off, she started to work on the ones that went in the other direction. Just as carefully she slid those off and laid the ribbons out on the basin top.

"Here goes, kiddo." Auntie got her fingers beneath one lid flap and pulled up. Stacks and stacks of Benjamin Franklin grinned up at us.

"There's more than twenty bills there. That's more than was in the lettuce ball," I said, looking over her shoulder. "That's more money than I've ever seen."

"Or are likely to see," Auntie agreed. She stroked the surface of the bills with her fingertips. "And they're all fresh and smooth. If they'd come from the ball of money, they would have been wrinkled."

"Let's check the numbers anyway," I suggested.

"Okay, kiddo." From her purse, Auntie took out her list and began to unfold it. "It'll go faster if you read while I check."

I bent over. "Check. I mean, right." And I read the first number to her.

"Nope," she said, "try another."

So I looked at the bill next to it and read the serial number.

"Hey, that's the same number you just gave me." Auntie leaned over and read a different bill. "So's this." She straightened. "It's counterfeit money. Good ones, though."

"That's why Uncle Leonard was so anxious to keep the box with him," I said breathlessly. "Do you think he printed all this up?"

Auntie stared at the piles of money. "No. He's probably a courier. He said he was supposed to meet someone. I bet it was to hand this over." She tapped her fingers against the money. "Ah Luke said he liked to gamble, so perhaps he's working off some gambling debt this way."

I rested against the wall. "Do we call the police?"

Auntie lowered the lid and eased its flaps back inside

the box. "Let me think." She chewed her lip as she worked the ribbons back over the box. When she was done, you couldn't have told that the box had ever been opened. "There," she said, making one final adjustment.

"So what'll we do?" I asked.

She hoisted the box. "We'll tell Leonard that we know what's in the box and give him a chance to turn himself in."

"And what if doesn't want to?"

Auntie had once bent the rules to help a group of sewing women who had been cheated out of their wages, but not this time. "Then we call Norm."

Norm was one of Auntie's actor clients, but his day-time job was in the district attorney's office.

However, when we returned to the bar, someone else had occupied Uncle Leonard's seat. "Where is he?" Auntie asked, looking all around.

"Oh, no. What if he's already left for his meeting?" I asked. "And we still haven't found Ann's two thousand. If it wasn't Lung, and it wasn't Uncle Leonard, then who was it?"

CHAPTER TWENTY-TWO

Auntie searched the crowd around the bar. There was a basketball game on the bar television. "We've got to get this to him. If he shows up with just a chocolate cake, they could hurt him. Those guys mean business."

"But how?" I asked, helping her look.

Auntie was already elbowing her way through the crowd at the bar. "I'll tell 'em I grabbed this by mistake."

At first the bartender was going to ignore her, concentrating instead on filling some orders. Desperately Auntie shoved between a seated couple and reached across the wooden counter to grab the bartender by the collar. "Where's the man who was on that stool?" She pointed to the place where Uncle Leonard had been.

"He went off with Jerry," the bartender gasped.

"So where's Jerry?" Auntie demanded.

The bartender was too busy trying to breathe to speak. Instead, he swung his eyes toward the kitchen.

Auntie let him go and whirled around. She grasped the box in both hands as she charged toward the doors.

Clasping her order pad, Debby suddenly got in Auntie's way. "Are you ready to order?" she asked.

"In a moment, honey." Auntie held up the box. "I've got to give this to a friend."

When Auntie nodded in the direction of the kitchen, Debby grew pale. "Oh, no, you can't go in there. You could get hit by a tray." Alarmed, she grasped Auntie's arm.

I wedged myself in between Debby and Auntie as if I was squeezing my way onto a bus. Before my momentum Debby was unable to keep her grip. "Go," I urged Auntie.

"You don't understand," Debby said, trying to stop Auntie.

I went into my basketball-guard stance to block her. "No, you're the one who doesn't understand."

As Auntie headed toward the kitchen, Debby called out, "Stop them, Jackie."

Jackie was a man in his thirties with a mustache. He looked puzzled at first, and then he saw Auntie heading straight toward the kitchen. "I'm sorry, madame, you can't—" he began to say.

His mistake was in assuming Auntie was just some plump, polite society matron from Pacific Heights. Auntie swung her hips as violently as she had when she had done those bone-cracking dances in *South Sea Siren*. (She'd caught pneumonia making that film, because she'd been clad only in a skimpy sarong on a drafty soundstage.) The resulting collision sent Jackie stumbling backward like a human eight ball, his arms waving around as he tried to regain his balance. He crashed onto a table where a couple had been digging into their desserts. Cream and rum custard flew everywhere in a wide circle of destruction.

As Jackie struggled to rise from the mess, Auntie paused long enough to call out, "Sorry. But at least it wasn't flambé."

I caught up with Auntie, pushing a hand against her back to urge her forward. "I'll run interference," I said, feeling just like Luke Skywalker's wing man in *Star Wars*.

I steered Auntie toward the kitchen, looking around the dining area, ready to stop any other waitron; but we didn't run into any trouble until we got to the doors.

Unfortunately, we didn't know at the time that the right door was used just for entering the kitchen and the left door was used only for exiting.

Hand thrust out like a halfback's, box tucked under her arm like a football, Auntie hit the left door. However, she picked the exact same moment that a waitron tried to swing the door outward. Through the large circular window in the door, I saw the back of her ponytailed head. She was trying to back through the doors while she held her tray in her arms. For a moment Auntie stood there pushing against a door that wouldn't budge.

"This way," I yelled, and I plunged through the right door.

When she saw me holding the door open for her, Auntie slid over in my direction. With Auntie no longer shoving the door from the outside, the poor waitron, who had been pushing from her side, fell into the dining area. For a horrifying moment the air was filled with baby carrots and parsley and mesquite chicken.

As the tray landed with a loud clang and the plates crashed to the floor, Auntie paused in the doorway. "Sorry," she said.

"You're going to have to leave a big tip," I said as I nudged her into the kitchen.

The kitchen was filled with big professional stoves. Huge pots simmered on some. Chefs in white hats and coats danced before others as they tossed things into pans. Clipped to the hood of one stove were the various orders in a neat row. To one side a couple of waitrons stood before a shelf filled with rows of salads. Everywhere there was steam or flames, so it seemed more like a factory manufacturing something than a kitchen making dinners. In one corner stood an elderly Chinese man at a big sink filled with stacks of dirty dishes, washing plates with a spray nozzle.

We were a couple of steps away from a plain brown door that suddenly banged open. I had assumed it was the door to a storage pantry, but Uncle Leonard himself stumbled backward out of the room. "I don't know what happened," he was saying.

"Over here," Auntie said, holding up the box.

Terrified, Uncle Leonard whirled around. He wasn't the elegant restaurateur now. His face was twisted by panic and covered by sweat.

"Come back inside my office," a fat man said. His considerable girth was covered by a snappy green suit, though he had rolled back the sleeves. He was reaching for Uncle Leonard with one hand while his other hand fished for something in one of the pockets of his coat.

Uncle Leonard stood, petrified. "I swear I didn't do it, Jerry."

I was just as frozen by the menace coming from the fat man. The whole kitchen was suddenly still as everyone stared at Jerry.

Auntie had had plenty of practice facing danger in the movies—even if it was only make-believe. She stepped right up to Uncle Leonard. "I'm so sorry, Leonard. Your box must have gotten mixed up with mine."

Uncle Leonard blinked but did not dare take his eyes off Jerry. "What?"

"You took my cake by mistake. This is your box." Auntie thrust it into his hands.

Uncle Leonard looked as if he could barely trust his ears. "My box?" When he saw it resting in his hand, he laughed nervously. "My box!" He raised his head with some of his old confidence. "I mean, your box." And he held it out to Jerry.

"Lady, how did you know it wasn't your cake? Did you look inside?" Jerry kept on coming. He moved in a heavy, forceful way that reminded me of a bulldozer. And he seemed to have found what he was looking for in his pocket.

Auntie spread out her arms. "I could tell by the difference in the weight. My box was very light."

I joined Auntie. If there was any danger, we'd face it together. "Yes, that bakery makes the best desserts."

Jerry put a hand on Uncle Leonard's shoulder. "I think we'd all better go back inside my office and talk." His hand, inside the coat pocket, twitched something blunt at us. I assumed he had a gun.

Uncle Leonard licked his lips nervously. "Jerry, I'll go back inside, but please leave them out of it."

"Everybody," Jerry grunted. He narrowed his small eyes into slits and smiled, enjoying the whole thing.

Auntie, though, had the presence of mind to snag Leonard's box by its ribbon. Pivoting like a crane, she swung the box out from Uncle Leonard's outstretched hands and over a stove burner. "Let him go, Jerry, or I'll drop this in the fire."

"Okay, okay. Don't get excited." Jerry released Uncle Leonard as if he himself was on fire.

Auntie held the box over the flames. "Now the three of us are going to leave. When we're outside, we'll leave this on the sidewalk."

"Sure, sure," Jerry licked his lips, like a cat watching a canary.

Auntie waved her free hand at Uncle Leonard. "Leonard, take my niece out."

"Auntie," I protested, but Uncle Leonard took my arm.

"Come on," he said, grabbing me. "She knows what she's doing."

I wish I could have been as confident as Uncle Leonard, and I didn't want to leave, but he was too strong. Slowly we began to move toward the swinging doors.

"I'll get you for this," Jerry growled. His eyes darted from side to side as Auntie slowly backed up toward us. With a speed that was amazing in such a big man, Jerry sprang to the sink. Snatching the nozzle from the dishwasher's hand, he hit the metal tab at the back of the sprayer and sent a spray of water arcing toward Auntie. Hot water splashed the floor at first and then swept toward her as he aimed the nozzle higher.

The silvery stream washed over her hand with such force that it sent her backward.

"I'll fix you now," Jerry growled, advancing as far as the nozzle would reach. Out of spite he sent the spray full into Auntie's face.

As she stood there gasping and spluttering, I grabbed the box from her hand.

"Give it to him," Uncle Leonard ordered frantically.

But I shoved an elbow into Jerry's stomach and slipped under his outstretched arm to dart into the dining area. The diners had given up any pretense of eating by then, and instead were gawking like bystanders at an accident.

I tried to remember everything Auntie had taught me about projecting my voice. "In recognition of our restaurant's anniversary, we are making a free gift of money!" From the way heads shot up, I knew they had heard me—even at the bar, over the noise of the televised game.

As I trotted into the dining area, I snatched up a knife from a table and desperately sawed at the ribbons.

"Come back here, kid," Jerry shouted. He had bulled past Auntie and Uncle Leonard and come through the other swinging door.

As the last ribbons parted, I yelled, "Money, free money." Dropping the knife, I opened the lid and threw a handful of bills into the air. The green rectangles fluttered in the air like leaves.

Instantly chairs crashed to the floor as people stood up

to grab at all the floating Benjamin Franklins.

"Money, free money," I said, scattering counterfeit bills as I scampered through the restaurant.

Jerry had given up any pretense of hiding his gun. He would have shot me, I think, but he had a horde of diners shoving and bumping him as they scrambled after the money. Thank heaven it was a popular restaurant.

The crowd was so intent on catching the money that they ignored Jerry, until out of sheer frustration he aimed his pistol at the ceiling and let loose a shot. The explosion echoed from the high ceiling and everyone froze.

"You're dead, kid," Jerry announced. People started to shout and scream as they ducked for cover. Oblivious of the panic, Jerry calmly took aim.

Suddenly Kong came from nowhere, slamming into the fat man's side. They went over together and crashed onto a table.

As Kong and Jerry wrestled on the floor, Uncle Leonard threw himself on them. A shot rang out. A glass cowboy-hat candleholder shattered, dumping the candle onto the tablecloth. Flames began to dance on the red and white squares.

Suddenly Uncle Leonard jerked Jerry's hand, still grasping the gun, up into the air. "Run, kids," Uncle Leonard ordered Kong and me frantically.

Kong, however, only rolled over to a table. Rising to his knees, he snatched a decorative cactus from a table. Then, twisting around, he brought it down hard. The painted pot landed with a solid thunk against Jerry's head.

Jerry's feet twitched once, and then he lay still.

All of a sudden the empty box felt like a ton in my hands, and I lowered them. If I had been a couple of inches closer to the table, the bullet would have hit me and not the candleholder. I suppose it was the reaction after having so much adrenaline pumping through me, but my arms and legs felt as weak as noodles. I sat down with a thump on the floor.

CHAPTER TWENTY THREE

"*W*hat *you doing here?*" I asked Kong as we headed for the front door. People were scrambling for the money again, so we had to maneuver around them.

Kong nearly tripped over a bald man who suddenly lunged after a counterfeit bill. "*We were wondering what happened to you when you didn't show up. Then Ah Luke came home and told us where you'd gone. He thought you might need some help.*"

Kong could be as spiny as a porcupine most of the time, but few people would have charged a man with a gun. "*I glad you came,*" I told him.

Suddenly he seemed all embarrassed. "*It wasn't for you. It was f-f-for the master,*" he stammered.

"*You don't have to pretend anymore,*" Auntie said from behind us. "*We like you. It's okay to like us.*"

"*I don't need any friends,*" Kong growled, but he seemed to be saying it more to himself than to us.

"For heaven's sake, talk English, will you?" Uncle

Leonard said from the rear.

"Don't you speak Chinese?" Auntie asked over her shoulder.

"Never needed to," Uncle Leonard said.

Lung was waiting outside with his face pressed to the plate-glass window. When he saw us, he opened the door so we could make our escape to the sidewalk.

Uncle Leonard set his hands on his hips. "Now would you mind telling me why you nearly got me killed with your fake box?"

Auntie patted her purse. "When you left the hospital, a hundred-dollar bill fluttered out of your pocket. It was one of the missing bills from Ann's stolen money."

Shock replaced anger. "Someone must've planted it on me." He spread his arms away from his sides. "Look. I don't have to steal from Ann. And I certainly wouldn't blow up my nephews. Ann didn't think it was me, did she?"

He sounded sincere.

"Ann didn't want to believe it," Auntie said.

I held up the pink box. "Do you mind telling us what were you doing with this?"

Uncle Leonard looked sheepish. "It was Jerry's full house to my three aces that got me into it. To settle the debt, I've been doing him favors. Among other things I was supposed to pick up that package and bring it to him. But I'm through with that." He held out his hand. "Give me the box."

"Why should we trust you?" I asked.

"Because Jerry makes me feel dirty. I'm going to the cops." Uncle Leonard went to a pay phone outside the restaurant and punched some buttons. A moment later he was talking with a 911 operator. When he was finished, he hung up, looking relieved.

Auntie nodded to me. "Give him the box."

Reluctantly, I handed the box over to Uncle Leonard, who tucked the lid flaps into the box. "You know, if you want to catch the thief, you might ask yourself who had the most to gain by having the restaurant fold."

"There was you," Auntie said bluntly.

Uncle Leonard winced. "You've got Ann's talent for going right for the jugular, but who else is a suspect besides me? I want to find out who hurt my nephews as much as you do. What about the school that lost the lion dance contest?"

I glanced at Kong, but he hadn't understood what we were saying.

"I think we can rule them out," Auntie said.

"It had to be someone who knew about the ball of money," Uncle Leonard said. He thought for a moment.

Auntie wagged an index finger. "Maybe we've been thinking too small. It isn't just the money at stake. Ann had to put the property up as collateral so she could open the restaurant. That's a valuable piece of property. If she fails to pay the loan, the bank gets the land."

"You can't suspect a banker." Uncle Leonard chuckled.

"Thanks to you, no reputable banker would go near Ann," Auntie said.

Uncle Leonard had the decency to blush. "So maybe it was a disreputable one. Did Ann say which bank loaned her the money?"

Auntie scratched her head. "I don't think she mentioned it."

I strained my memory, trying to remember. "Did she even say it was a bank?"

Auntie snapped her fingers. "No, come to think of it."

"Maybe it was a loan shark." Uncle Leonard handed Auntie a quarter. "I'd check if I were you. Ann's probably still at the hospital. Just don't tell her about this part of the evening."

Auntie took the quarter. "She's going to find out soon anyway. I bet Ann would help you if you asked her to."

He grimaced. "Ann hates me."

"She won't after I tell her how you tried to save us from Jerry."

Uncle Leonard sighed in relief. "Thanks."

Auntie had to call Information to get Wesleyan's number, and then it took a few minutes to get through to Barry's room. Auntie looked thoughtful when she hung up the phone. "It was a private company. Empire Enterprises."

"I'd start with Empire Enterprises for suspects," Uncle Leonard said.

In the distance we could all hear the sirens screaming. The sound made both Lung and Kong nervous. *"No police,"* Kong said in Chinese.

"No, no police," Auntie agreed, taking a card and pen from her purse. *"Why don't you go back to Lung's room? Do you know the number of the pay phone in the hallway?"* she asked Lung.

As the sirens grew closer, Lung hastily scribbled it on the back of the card and then returned the card and pen to Auntie.

Auntie took their father's journal from her purse. *"And thanks,"* she said, handing it to Lung.

Lung looked at Kong as he clutched it. *"You're right. They're not bad for native-born."*

"You not bad for foreign-born," I said.

Kong grinned and wiggled his hand. I interpreted that as a friendly wave, so I waved back. With a nod Kong and his brother hurriedly turned around and began walking away.

"Those are kids with guts," Uncle Leonard said. "Friends of yours?" He must not have recognized Kong from the kitchen fight.

"Yeah, I guess they are," I said, watching them leave. It wasn't going to be easy being Kong's friend, but he had saved my life twice now. When someone does that, you can learn to overlook his shortcomings, and maybe I had work to do on my own point of view too.

Auntie dialed Information again. "There's no listing for Empire Enterprises," she said.

"Rather odd for a business that invests money, wouldn't you say?" Uncle Leonard asked.

"It's more than odd. It stinks," Auntie said. "But how do we find out more about them?"

"I know. We need Akeem. He can find out anything on his computer," I said, and I turned to Uncle Leonard. "Can you lend us cab fare?"

Uncle Leonard took out a slim leather wallet and

184

extracted a couple of twenties. "And these are the genuine thing. How far are you going?"

"Just over to Russian Hill," I said.

There were enough taxis cruising the area to make finding one easy. As we got in, a patrol car pulled in to the curb. Uncle Leonard started walking toward the car, holding the box in front of him.

"Do you think he was lying?" I asked Auntie.

"He's a skunk, but I think he likes to do his fighting in court," Auntie said. "The trouble is, almost anyone could have slipped the hundred-dollar bill into his pocket to try to frame him. Everyone in the business knows about his feud with Ann. He was an easy target to set up as a suspect. We're dealing with someone smarter and more subtle than a street gang."

I gave the cabby Akeem's address, and he drove over the hills. That evening the entire city seemed to be covered by a blanket of fog. Windows glowed like yellow eyes from the lower floors, but the windows of the upper floors were only will-o'-the-wisps. The few pedestrians were bundled up against the damp and the cold. It was a sad, sleepy time—a time to curl up in bed with a cup of hot chocolate and a book with a happy ending.

Akeem's house was on a street so steep that the cabby had to put the taxi into a lower gear, and as it crept up the slope, the cab grumbled to itself like an elderly giant.

"This is it," I said, as the cab stopped in front of one of those prefab boxes that sprout up instantly like mushrooms.

On the left side of the apartment doorway was an

intercom covered by a metal plate and some wire mesh to speak through. Underneath were buttons with names neatly printed next to them.

I found Akeem's and buzzed the flat. When there wasn't any answer, I stepped to the edge of the sidewalk. The light was definitely on in his flat, so I buzzed again. It took several tries before I heard Akeem's irritated voice over the intercom.

Akeem sounded as if we were pulling his teeth out. "Go away. I'm busy," he growled.

Good old Akeem. He was the best hacker in our school, but he had all the social skills of rock moss. But Barry was his best friend as well as his partner in the lion dance. I knew he would help.

I leaned forward and pressed the button again. "It's me, Lily," I said.

Akeem ran true to form. "You're bothering me."

"Just trying to be friendly," I said defensively. "I need to talk to you. I've got a big favor to ask. Can we come up?"

"Tomorrow," he snarled. "I'm trying to find out what I can on Master Wang."

"We don't think it's the master," I said. "We think someone else is the thief and bomber."

"Why didn't you say so in the first place?" he asked, annoyed.

He buzzed us through the front door.

"Akeem?" I called. My voice echoed up the stairwell.

His response floated down to us dimly. "Up here on the top floor—all ready to catch the thief."

I led Auntie up the metal steps to the upper floor,

where Akeem had left his front door open. "Come on in," he called.

Akeem's mother had died when he was small, so it was just he and his father, and their flat was as cold and impersonal as they both were. Shining steel shelves, crammed with electronic gear, hid the walls, and the furniture was all black leather.

Through the large picture window in the living room the bay was visible, its waters black as ink, and beyond that the slopes of the East Bay, the tiny lights glittering like gold dust that covered the hills.

However, Akeem was oblivious to the lovely view. He sat at a desk that had been set up in a corner of the living room. On it was a computer.

He barely glanced at us before his eyes returned to the computer screen. "So who are we looking for?"

"It's not so much who as what." I sat on an edge of the desk as I filled him in quickly on the suspicious Empire Enterprises. "Can you find out anything on them?" I asked.

"Of course I can," he said. "It may sound difficult to someone like you, but it's child's play to me." Though he knew everything there was to know about computers, part of him reminded me of a small boy who liked to pinch ears.

Auntie had been more fascinated by the framed photos on the wall than the computer screen. "It's better to think some things than to say them out loud," she said in the sweet, calm voice that she might use with a naughty three-year-old.

He tilted back his head, curious. "Really?"

Auntie indicated some photos that showed Akeem before the Taj Mahal and other famous places. "You've been more places than there are in an atlas."

Akeem put his hands behind his head and shrugged. "And never long enough in any one place to get to know anyone."

I pointed at a photo of Akeem's father in his navy uniform. "Why—did your father keep getting reassigned?"

"It's what happens when you can do something that no one else can." Akeem couldn't keep the pride from his voice.

Auntie timidly examined the computer on the desk. "Well, I admit computers are foreign to me. Are you allowed to use your father's computer?"

"This is mine." Akeem touched the machine with almost a caress. "I learned how to use computers from the time I could sit on his lap. When he worked at home on his computer, he always let me watch him, and he always answered my questions." A grin flashed across his face and then disappeared as quickly as it started. "He's got a lot more patience than I've got."

I figured everyone did. He'd bite off the head of anyone who asked him the simplest things. I knew from experience that had to be true.

Auntie folded her arms. "If you told me I had to sacrifice a chicken to start the computer, I would. I don't know anything about them."

He chuckled. "Neither does your niece. I remember that time she almost lost our term paper."

I started to defend myself, but Auntie turned to me so

he couldn't see her face as she raised and lowered her eyebrows. I shut up. "Were you able to retrieve it?" she asked, sympathizing with Akeem.

Auntie didn't know Akeem the way I did. "After a lot of complaining and scolding," I said, punching him in the arm. "He's worse than my dad when I try to get him to drive me somewhere. What a grouch."

"It takes one to know one," he shot back. "Time to get cracking."

Swinging around, he hunched over the keyboard. The silvery light flickered across his face as his fingers danced over the keys. "Interesting," he murmured as he studied the screen. His fingers clicked down in a quick rhythm, and more names scrolled across the computer. "Empire Enterprises seem to be a lot of dummy holding companies." He smiled, enjoying the challenge.

"It's like those Russian nesting dolls," Auntie murmured. "You find one inside another."

Akeem cracked his knuckles. "They won't escape me," he said smugly.

"Take no prisoners," I urged, getting into the spirit of things.

It took another half hour before he had a name for us. "As far as I can tell, it's a C. M. Tang." With a flourish he punched a button. On another table a printer began rattling. He waved his hand toward it. "There's your hard copy."

I got the paper. "This address is just a mailbox in Chinatown. That's it?"

His eyes flicked toward me and then back to screen.

"You're welcome," he grunted.

I gave him a quick hug. "Thanks. You're a real pal."

He tried unsuccessfully to hide that he was pleased. "I am, aren't I?" And then as if he was afraid he had admitted too much, he shouldered me away. "Now beat it, and go find out who hurt Barry. I'll keep trying to do what I can on my end and get something more on Empire. Don't slam the door on the way out."

He was another human porcupine, but I was glad he was on our side.

It was too late to check out the mailbox, and Auntie and I were dog tired.

We used Leonard's money to take another cab and go home. I didn't think either of us would get much sleep, but as soon as my head hit the pillow, I drifted into dreams of huge lions dancing among flames.

had expected to find C. M. Tang's mailbox to be a fake, so I was surprised the next morning to find that it was in a store that provided all sorts of mailing services—mailers, cards, UPS and a dozen other possibilities. Looking through the window, I could see banks of little brass-plated doors filling one wall. Mailers and flattened boxes filled racks against the opposite wall.

At the rear of the store, sitting behind the counter, was a woman with green-frosted hair.

I looked harder at the little brass doors on the wall and saw that they each had numbers. "C. M. Tang probably gets the mail in one of those."

"Did you ever see *Here Comes Tiger Lil?*" Auntie asked me in a low voice.

"No," I confessed, hoping Auntie wouldn't take offense. "That one isn't on videotape." I knew from Mom that in it Auntie had tried to track down an orphan who had inherited a fortune.

"Well, watch me do a scene from it." Auntie adjusted

her coat and then lifted her head a bit as she marched across the red carpet and up to the counter. "Excuse me. Do you know a C. M. Tang?"

The woman looked up from her Chinese newspaper. "Nope."

"But I was told this was the address." Auntie produced an envelope from her purse and waved it about. She turned apparently with a sudden inspiration. "Perhaps it's one of those mailboxes."

"I can't tell you that," the clerk turned a page, careful not to tear the thin paper. "It's supposed to be confidential."

"But I've been looking for years," Auntie said. "I want to settle my debts. And I've heard that there's an illness in the family, and the money could be useful."

Auntie went on talking, creating a pretty good tearjerker that almost had me crying: misunderstandings and family feuds that kept lovers apart. If that was part of the plot to her movie, I hoped they'd get it on videotape pretty soon.

The clerk, though, was unmoved, turning the pages of the paper all the time while Auntie poured her heart out. She had all the makings of a movie critic.

"Please help me," Auntie finished. "I could be your mother."

Though her head was still bowed over her newspaper, the clerk's eyes flicked up to stare at Auntie skeptically.

"Or grandmother," Auntie added feebly. She hated saying that.

The clerk put an elbow on the counter and rested

her cheek against her palm. "You really want to see C. M. Tang?"

"Of course," Auntie said.

"You were standing right near her." The clerk turned the newspaper so we could see the article she had been reading. Though I couldn't read Chinese very well, I could tell from the headline that it was about Barry's accident. Above it was a photo of the restaurant opening. Watching the lion dance were Auntie, Ann, Morgan, me and Uncle Leonard, among others in the crowd.

"Which one is she?" Auntie asked intently.

The clerk gave Auntie a funny look and tapped a nail on Bernie's picture as she looked over Auntie's shoulder.

"That's impossible!" I said.

The clerk shrugged and began to read the next article. "She comes in every day, and she always gets lots of mail."

Auntie was thoughtful. "Would Akeem be at the computer this early?" she asked me.

"As long as there's electricity," I said.

"Let's pay him another visit, kiddo," Auntie said.

"Should I tell her you were looking for her?" the clerk asked.

"I'd appreciate it if you wouldn't," Auntie said quickly.

The clerk looked triumphant. "I didn't think it was a bad debt. Who are you really?"

Apparently the photo wasn't captioned. I might have told her she was talking to a world-famous actor, Tiger Lil, but Auntie was already spinning out another cover story.

"What would you say," she asked, "if I said I was from the city real estate board?"

"I knew it," the clerk said. "Is it like tipping off the I.R.S.? Do informants get a percentage of the penalties?"

I don't think Auntie had any idea what she meant, but she managed to sound brusquely confident anyway. "Three percent. Still, it could be a tidy sum."

"I bet it is," the clerk said excitedly. "She gets a lot of mail. Mostly from real estate agencies and big investment companies."

Sweet old Bernie? I couldn't believe it. The clerk seemed very sure, though. Auntie had the clerk write down her name and telephone number, and she put it away with a curt, professional nod.

Auntie turned and began to walk out. As I followed her, I couldn't help asking over my shoulder, "What happened to confidentiality?"

The clerk pulled out a calculator from underneath the counter. "It's not like I took an oath," she said. "And anyway, shouldn't we all help our government?" She began to calculate what three percent of various sums would buy her.

Outside, I shook my head. Yesterday it was human porcupines like Kong and Akeem who were all prickles on the outside but sweet on the inside. And now Bernie might be sweet on the outside and all sharp on the inside. "Do you think Bernie could really be C. M. Tang?"

"If she is, I'm glad she didn't turn to acting. We would've been competing for the same roles," Auntie said.

I still didn't want to believe it was Bernie. "So what do

we do, then? We can't just accuse her. I mean, what if she's innocent?"

Auntie thought for a moment. "Chinatown's still a small world. I bet the waiters and waitresses all know one another. Let's ask Ah Luke if he knows her."

We walked down Clay Street, past the alley that led to Cameron House, which was run by the Presbyterians and had a lot of social activities for kids. Auntie herself had gone there when she was young. "Had my first kiss there, kiddo." She winked. "And got thrown out right after that."

"What happened to the boy?" I teased.

Auntie sighed. "He died in W. W. Two." That was Auntie's shorthand for World War Two.

"I'm sorry," I said, and I left Auntie to her own thoughts. Chinatown was full of ghosts for Auntie, and she seemed to have a story for every square foot of it.

However, when we reached the corner of Stockton and Clay, it was impossible for Auntie to stay lost in her memories.

We met so many of Auntie's acquaintances that it took a half hour to cross the street. To the east of Stockton lay the heart of old Chinatown, and there were dozens of people buying food at the delis or the greengrocers'. Most of them had something to say to Auntie—usually the latest bit of gossip—and Auntie listened to them all, shaking her head in sympathy whenever it was appropriate.

Though Lung and Ah Luke's apartment was only a couple of blocks away, it took us another hour to get there because of Auntie's friends. We entered the dim, smelly tenement. It stank like the medicinal herbs my Mom brewed.

When we got to his room, Auntie knocked. "Ah Luke?"

Ah Luke looked embarrassed when he opened the door. He was dressed only in a T-shirt and pants. *"Lung, it's Tiger Lil for you."*

Kong was there too, and besides the two boys there were several other elderly men inside the room. It made me wonder where Kong had slept last night. On the floor?

"What did you find out?" Kong demanded. I saw Lung crowding up behind him.

"In a moment," Auntie said. *"Good to see you again,"* she said to Ah Luke.

One of the elderly men elbowed past the boys to stare at Auntie. *"I've seen all your films,"* he gushed, wiping his hands hastily on his pants. *"What are you doing here?"*

"I needed to talk with my friend," Auntie said, nodding to Ah Luke.

The man was obviously impressed, and he chided Luke. *"You never told me you knew anyone famous."*

Ah Luke shrugged. *"You never asked, Mr. Lee."*

"By the way, do you know a waitress by the name of Bernie?" Auntie spoke Chinese except for her American name.

"I know a Tang Chung Ming," Ah Luke said, giving her Chinese name. In Chinese her last name would have come first, but if you were writing it out in English, you would use Chung Ming Tang—or her initials, C. M. Tang. *"She also goes by the name of Bernice or Bernie."*

Mr. Lee laughed. *"That one wouldn't be seen with the likes of us."*

So they did know Bernie. "Why?" I asked.

From the way everyone guffawed, you would have thought I'd told the funniest joke. *"Because"*—Ah Luke chuckled—*"she owns this place."*

"And five more like it," Mr. Lee said.

"So she rich?" I said, amazed.

"And you better be on time with the rent," Ah Luke added.

"That's how she got rich," Mr. Lee said. *"She's the meanest woman alive. Saved all of her tips. Then she'd loan the money out at ridiculously high rates. Never shared a penny with her family."*

"Bernie?" I asked, still wanting to believe that nice woman was innocent.

"If she could, she'd charge us for the air we breathe," Ah Luke said.

"And I offered to help her get a job," Auntie muttered to me.

One of the other men reached past Mr. Lee to poke Ah Luke in the ribs. When Ah Luke turned, the man whispered in his ear. *"Would you mind meeting my roommates?"* Ah Luke asked Auntie.

"Not at all," Auntie assured him.

"Would you mind stepping outside? We'll be right out," he said.

Auntie looked puzzled, but she said, *"Sure."*

When Kong and Lung had stepped into the hallway with us, he shut the door.

"What did you find out?" Lung asked.

Auntie asked, "Lung, when you heard that voice on the phone telling you what to write in the notes, how did it sound?" She lowered her voice so she spoke gruffly. "Like this?"

Lung scratched his head. "I guess it could have been a woman."

So we told him briefly about Akeem's discoveries. We'd barely finished when Ah Luke came out of the room dressed in a freshly pressed suit. He headed a procession of five other men, every one of them dressed in a suit that he had put on just for the occasion. They nodded their heads shyly as Ah Luke introduced each of them.

Auntie had this funny ability that she must have developed in Hollywood. She could turn on the charm that lit up the dim hallway like a searchlight.

The elderly men became as excited as small boys as they began to talk about the movies they had seen—a couple of men who could not speak English had had to have someone translate the dialogue for them. They were impressed by Auntie, such a famous actor. Soon, though, the reminiscing widened to include the theaters they had gone to, all of them long since vanished from San Francisco.

I could see that they enjoyed remembering, and I could also see that Auntie got as much pleasure as they did.

"What's your next movie going to be?" one of them asked.

"Maybe a TV show," she said, with an airy wave of her hand.

By this time curious people in other rooms had opened their doors. They joined the group around Auntie. They were mostly elderly men like Ah Luke's group, but there were also some families, and elderly women too. They were drawn by the noise.

All of them hung on to Auntie's every word, and I could see the difference in the way she held her head up. It was like watching a battery get charged up with new energy. I guessed that Kong realized he'd been in the presence of a true celebrity.

Whether Bernie was a dead end to our investigation or not, I was glad we'd come here. I was so close to Auntie that sometimes I forgot what she meant to other people.

"So did you find the thief?" Ah Luke asked finally.

Auntie sighed reluctantly as she looked around at the crowd. "Maybe we should talk in private."

"The rest of you stay here," Ah Luke said to the crowd. Along with Kong and Lung, we followed him down the hallway until there was some distance between us and the crowd.

"Now, what did you discover?" he asked in a low voice.

So Auntie whispered to Ah Luke. She told him about our adventures. "We're not sure, of course. Do you think she's capable of doing those things?"

Ah Luke rubbed his chin. "There's one way to find out for sure."

"How?" Auntie asked.

"It was in your own movie Killer Cook," Ah Luke said. "You called up the suspect and pretended you knew his crimes and asked for blackmail money. Do the same with Bernie. If she comes and offers you money, you know she's guilty."

"That ended in a fight, as I recall," Auntie said. "My

stunt double broke two ribs."

"I'll call the realtor who collects our rent," Ah Luke offered. "He can pass the message on to her."

Auntie considered that, but finally she shook her head. "It's too dangerous. Bernie—or whoever it is—tried to run us over in a van. This isn't a movie."

However, it was impossible to dampen Ah Luke's optimism. "You can be nearby in disguise," he suggested. "I'm sure someone will lend you some clothes."

"Maybe we can borrow some clothes too," Lung said, glancing at Kong, who nodded his head.

"I can't let you do this," Auntie protested to Ah Luke.

Ah Luke looked at Auntie sternly. "When the boss died, I promised him I'd take care of his family. What will I say after I die and meet the boss? That I let someone mangle his grandsons and get away with it? You can't keep me away."

"She tried to dishonor my school," Kong said. "I want some of her."

"She disgraced me and my family," Lung added. "I'll be there too."

CHAPTER TWENTY-FIVE

Until I got outside, I hadn't realized how much the herbal medicine smell had deadened my nose. I took in deep drafts of the fresh air.

Auntie was holding up the collar of her borrowed coat to sniff. "Can you smell herbs?" she asked. Ah Luke's neighbor, Mrs. Chou, had been enthusiastic about lending me and the famous Tiger Lil some clothes.

"I think it's in our nostrils," I said, adjusting Mrs. Chou's tam. It had been knitted from brown wool with red and white stripes. It made me feel as if I was wearing a cap made out of chocolate candy.

Auntie sniffed the back of her hand and then her sleeve. "I'd swear it's all over us."

"I just hope it works for the owner as powerfully as it smells," I said. We started to cross Clay Street.

I guessed that the garage beneath Portsmouth Square must have filled up, because there was a long line of cars waiting to get in, curling around two sides of the block. A curving stone bridge linked the hotel across the street with the square.

Across the street Ah Luke had already sat down on a bench. Kong and Lung were on the next bench, wearing long cloth coats. Scarves covered their heads. Auntie had taken longer to put on her disguise because she had been far fussier than the two boys.

When Ah Luke saw us, he beckoned for us to come over.

Auntie caught me. "You're striding. Shuffle." Clasping her hands behind her back, she slid her feet along. "Remember, you're playing a role now."

There was applause from the doorway in back of us. The whole building had turned out to watch. They thought it was a rehearsal for a movie. *"Thank you,"* Auntie said, *"but I'll have to ask you to go back inside and not peek out. There mustn't be anything out of the ordinary."*

There was a hastily whispered conversation, and then the door closed to a narrow crack.

As Auntie waved her thanks, I stretched my arms behind me; but when I tried to clutch at my wrist, I grasped only nylon sleeve. My borrowed coat hung on me like an oversize tent.

Auntie eyed me critically while I tried a few steps. "Hmm, better keep behind me." Taking a scarf from her pocket, she began to tie it around her neck.

I made a last-minute adjustment to the knot holding the scarf tied around her head. "Do you think she'll come?"

Auntie studied her reflection in the side mirror of a parked car, and then, with a grunt of satisfaction, she slowly bent forward to lean upon the cane we had also borrowed. In the blink of an eye I was staring at a little old lady.

"The next thing I know, you'll be elbowing me out of the way at the fruit stall," I said admiringly.

"'In the quest after the perfect orange, no excess is wrong.'" Auntie slowly tapped her way across the sidewalk toward the street.

I did my best to move beside her, trying to remember everything I knew about acting, which consisted of a few minutes of coaching from Norm when we had once both been cans of Lion Salve in a parade: Mainly it was to be the best of whatever you were pretending to be.

I had just decided to pretend I was a rich woman whose crummy husband had stolen all her money when a small pickup truck ground to a halt, and the driver tooted its horn.

The Chinese driver wore an Oakland A's cap and had a thin little mustache that formed a scraggly V on his upper lip. Smiling, he waved for us to cross.

I bobbed my head in gratitude, and I pretended to support Auntie as I crossed the street. I wished she would walk faster, but by now Auntie was in character, so she hobbled along more slowly than a snail.

Behind the truck, traffic was building up, and a delivery truck driver finally began tooting his horn. Our driver remained unruffled, though, and he sat behind the wheel as if he was prepared to wait the whole day if he had to.

I breathed a sigh of relief as we stepped up onto the curb. In back of us came a toot, and I waved back to the truck driver as he began to chug down Clay Street. Following him was a long procession of cars, vans, delivery trucks and tourist buses, clinging to one another's bumpers like a line of mechanical elephants holding on to one another's tails.

I turned around and saw the crowded fire escapes of Ah Luke's tenement. All the inhabitants had gathered up there to watch the "movie" spectacle. Besides being dangerous, it also defeated our purpose, so I waved for them to go back inside. It took a couple of tries before they finally got the hint and climbed back through the windows into their apartments.

There were about fifty elderly Chinese women scattered around the benches of the Square and twice as many Chinese men clustered around the game tables. Cooing around the square, pigeons strutted as they looked for scraps. Dad always called them feathered rats.

Ah Luke sat on the bench, glancing around at the crowd. *"Don't look at me,"* Auntie whispered as we passed him.

"Yes, yes, I know," he said, making a point of looking everywhere but in our direction. With a great show he pulled a folded-up Chinese newspaper from his pocket and spread it open to read.

We eased down upon a bench to his left, within earshot. Then we settled down to wait. Around us a hundred conversations merged into a sea of voices, ebbing and flowing rhythmically like a tide. When one of the chess players made a particularly good move, some of the voices rose loudly in approval. As I sat there, I felt like

I was floating on an ocean.

Auntie, though, brought me back to reality. "Don't slouch," she muttered to me. She herself was sitting, leaning upon her cane.

I made myself sit up erect. "Like this?"

She glanced at me from the corner of her eye. "It'll have to do."

The problem with cop shows is they never show you the boring parts. We waited on those benches for hours. When Kong and Lung started to grow impatient, they began wagging their legs back and forth until Auntie shot them a stern look. Near sunset my rear began to ache. The bench began to feel like it was made out of iron.

I was wondering if Bernie would show when Auntie whispered, "Here she comes."

I looked for her, but all I saw was a tourist lady entering the square from Washington Street. It took me a moment to realize it was Bernie. She wasn't wearing her usual uniform but a fur-trimmed coat, worn open to show a simple but elegant dress. Her hair had been piled on top of her head.

"She's wearing an Armani," Auntie murmured with admiration.

"That's expensive?" I asked.

"Ah Luke would have to work three months or more to earn that," Auntie explained. "And that wouldn't cover the Italian shoes and the Gucci bag."

Bernie stood for a moment and surveyed the Square through her sunglasses, looking as if she wished she was anywhere but here.

I tried hard not to let my jaw drop in astonishment. "Are you sure that's not her evil twin sister?"

Auntie said a little jealously, "She's not a bad actor."

Ah Luke lowered his newspaper and waved to her. With a slight nod she walked toward him impatiently, heels clicking on the pavement.

"*How much?*" she asked.

Ah Luke deliberately folded up the newspaper. "*How much for what?*"

Bernie took off her dark glasses, flicking the earpiece down with a twist of her wrist. "*How much for keeping your mouth shut?*"

Carefully, Ah Luke slid the newspaper into a pocket. "*Shut about what?*"

She glared at Ah Luke. "*Did you or did you not send me the message? My agent said it was you.*"

Ah Luke adjusted his lapels with great dignity. "*I did. I have many expenses.*" He gazed at Bernie. "*And I think you have a good deal of money.*"

Bernie shifted from foot to foot as she began to negotiate. "*I have my expenses too.*"

"*I think I could forget a good deal if I could have some of the hundred-dollar bills you stole,*" Ah Luke said. "*Let's say five of them.*"

Bernie hesitated and then opened her purse. "*All right.*" She slipped out some bills. They had a lot of creases. I would have bet anything that they were from the money that had been folded up into the lettuce ball.

Ah Luke took the money and began to count it.

"*Don't do that here, you idiot,*" Bernie snapped.

Ah Luke went on counting, though. *"This will do for this month."*

"That's all." Bernie snapped her purse shut.

Ah Luke eyed her scornfully. *"You always were stingy. Even when we worked in the same restaurant thirty years ago."*

Bernie looked away edgily. *"You were an idiot then, and you still are. I scrimped and saved every penny I ever got."*

"And never helped your friends and family," Ah Luke said.

"We're in America now," Bernie insisted, full of excuses. *"It's everyone for themselves."*

"Why did you hurt my boss's grandsons?" Ah Luke slipped the money into a pocket.

"I didn't mean to," Bernie said defensively. *"I only wanted to blow the fake ball up in the kitchen on the table, but the fuses must have fizzled. I didn't know they'd go off outside and hurt anyone. I was just trying to cover my tracks."*

Ah Luke did his best to control his anger. *"What did those poor boys ever do to you? Don't you have enough money? Ms. Fisher was kind to you."*

Bernie lifted her head self-righteously. *"It was her father, our former boss. He borrowed a thousand dollars from me. He swore he'd pay me, but he never did. And when he died, his wife refused to honor the debt. But his family owed me."* The self-righteous outrage crept into her voice. Even now Bernie couldn't get over the betrayal. *"And yet Chinatown thinks they're so virtuous and wonderful."*

I thought about the threatening notes. That's what they had meant by "honour the debt." This was the other side of that Chinatown tradition of paying what you owed.

Obviously, collecting what was owed to you was equally important. Only collecting for Bernie had grown into a full-blown Chinatown feud, and her resentment was as deep as her memory was long.

"*Did you have a signed IOU?*" Ah Luke demanded.

Bernie stared ahead of her, as if she was deep in her memories now. "*I had his word. That should have been enough.*"

"*As you said, this is America. You need a signed note.*" Ah Luke rubbed his cheek. "*Why didn't you get one?*"

"*Everyone said he was so honorable,*" Bernie said bitterly. "*So I decided I would get his family to pay me one way or another. It took almost twenty years, but I got it from the daughter. With interest. Two thousand instead of one thousand.*"

And possibly a valuable property, if the restaurant went under too. Not a bad haul.

Ah Luke suddenly wagged an index finger at her. "*Now I understand why you didn't ask for an IOU. You didn't want anything in writing that the tax people could find.*"

"*The government takes enough of my money,*" Bernie said.

Ah Luke studied her. "*I wondered how you could buy all that property when you were young. How much of your tips were you declaring to the IRS? And how many undeclared profits on loans?*"

Bernie drew herself up huffily. "*That's my business.*"

"*That will cost you extra,*" Ah Luke said.

Her eyes narrowed in warning. "*No one likes a greedy pig.*"

Ah Luke settled back. "*I understand the government gives*

a percentage to the informer when they catch a tax cheat."

Bernie sucked in her breath sharply. It was strange to watch her face change. There was still the same wide smile, but it was stiff now, and there was a malicious look to her face. It was almost like looking at a giant evil doll. "*Accidents can happen again—especially if you get greedy,*" she warned.

I would have been afraid, but Ah Luke regarded her calmly. "*Are you going to blow me up too?*"

"*There are plenty of things that can happen to an old fool.*" Bernie licked her lips, as if she was enjoying the possibilities. Maybe she was imagining a van running him over.

"I think that's enough," Auntie said. Pulling off her bandanna, she nodded to Kong and Lung. They rose from a nearby bench, glad to shed the scarves that covered their heads.

"*It's going to be fun watching you go to jail.*" Kong grabbed her left arm while his brother grasped her right.

"*It was my money,*" Bernie said, and she twisted free from the two boys, who looked surprised. I don't think either of them had expected her to struggle.

Bernie shoved Kong into Lung, and the two of them fell over the bench on top of Ah Luke.

Somehow, when we had been planning this, no one had foreseen this part. I stepped in front of Bernie and stretched out my arms. "Stop in the name of the IRS" was the first thing that came to my head.

On all the police shows on television they never show you this part, with the suspect charging straight at you like a crazy bull either. Bernie's clothes and jewelry couldn't disguise the fact that she had the basic shape and mass of a steamroller. I had one moment to see her angry face and the purse clutched in her hands; and the next moment she had bowled me over.

I thought Auntie would try to stop her next, but she just stood. "It's no use, Bernie. By the time the IRS is finished with you, you won't have a penny left," she said.

Bernie jabbed a ringed finger at Auntie. "You old has-been. Don't even think about trying to stop me."

"Not without a stunt double," Auntie said amiably.

Bernie took in Auntie's disguise. "At least you're finally dressing your age," she snorted, and she started past.

With the precision of an all-star pitcher, Auntie swung her purse up to hit Bernie, but the strap broke. I think Auntie's overworked purse just wore out from the strain. Instead of knocking Bernie in the head, the purse flew between Bernie's legs. Poor purse. It had given its all. But it still did the trick.

Bernie sprawled face forward with an angry yell, and Auntie plopped down on her back like a human paper-weight. "Has-been indeed," she said, sniffing.

CHAPTER TWENTY-SIX

"**A**untie, you already had three helpings," I whispered.

Auntie paused with the platter in her hand. "Bernie almost threw me off because I was so light. I think there's such a thing as going too far with a diet." She spooned more of Ann's special chicken onto her plate, even though the sauce was heavy with honey.

Auntie was going off her diet with a vengeance. I nudged her in the side. "But what about Clark's show? What about Hollywood?"

Auntie returned the platter to the large lazy Susan on the table. "I've had time to think. I'm finished with ingenue roles. I think it's time I moved on to character parts. There's always a demand for a good character actor."

"You important, you got flesh," Ah Luke agreed from across the table. I didn't point out that he himself was thin as a skeleton.

"Let her eat. It's a compliment to the restaurant," Barry said softly. Even after he'd gotten out of the hospital, he'd kept some of the confidence he had won in the lion dance contest.

He and Scott were lending a hand waiting on tables and busing the dirty plates. The restaurant was a big success, and the boys were needed this Saturday evening.

"You're really busy," I said, looking around at the crowded restaurant.

"You should have seen it at lunch," Barry said with quiet pride.

"How're the eyes?" Auntie asked him.

"Good enough to see my brother when he's loafing." Barry laughed.

"Who's loafing? Come on, Barry. Set up table ten. We've got people waiting." Scott was hopping around a nearby table, setting down napkins, plates, cups and chopsticks.

"Okay, okay," Barry said. "Can't I talk to my friends for a moment?"

Scott prodded Barry. "Not when there are paying customers waiting."

"How's the arm?" I asked.

"It'll be good as new in a week," Scott said. "I should be able to play."

Barry waved as Scott dragged him through the swinging doors into the kitchen.

"I hear Leonard will be out on parole in a month," Auntie said to Ah Luke. "Do you think he'll be running Ciao Chow again?"

"I don't think so. The new manager his mother picked out is working out just fine." Ah Luke added by way of explanation, "He listens to me."

"And Kong and Lung?" I asked.

Uncle Leonard had arranged for them to be hired at the Ciao Chow.

"They're working out fine too. Quick to learn." Ah Luke sipped his tea. "I'm teaching them English now."

Barry and Scott reappeared, holding the doors open so Ann could come out. She was wearing a short white jacket, and her hair was hidden inside a white chef's hat. Behind her was Morgan, holding a tray in his hands.

"I know you're not ready for dessert yet," Ann said, "but I wanted to present these while there was a break."

Auntie leaned over curiously. "I didn't know you had added desserts to the menu."

"We didn't. Ann made these special for you." Morgan bent forward so we could see the bite-size chocolate éclairs.

I leaned forward to look at the decorations on top of them. "You put lion dancers on them."

"That's because you're the true lion," Barry said to Auntie.

"With a lion-sized appetite," Auntie agreed.

By the time this evening was over, I thought, Auntie would definitely be finished with ingenue roles.

"Each of these has a different filling." Ann began to point. "This one is rum, this one mocha . . ."

With each new item, Auntie's eyes glistened, and when Ann was finished, Auntie deftly liberated the tray from her hands. "That's far too heavy to carry back to the kitchen. Why don't you leave these here?"

"We were thinking about adding a small bakery

counter," Ann said. "What do you think?"

"I'd say a bakery counter would be a big hit," I said, hastily clearing a space for the tray.

Morgan looked around the restaurant. Everyone was watching us. Some customers had even gotten out of their chairs to get a better peek at the tray. "It might at that."

Auntie set the tray down in front of her. "You can hang up a sign: EAT DESSERT FIRST. LIFE IS UNCERTAIN."

Ann laughed as she spread out her hands. "In the meantime, enjoy."

"That we will," Auntie promised, surveying the tray for her first target. "Oh, boy."

"You have to share, Auntie," I warned her.

"But I get first choice," she insisted, rubbing her hands gleefully.

LAURENCE YEP grew up in San Francisco, where he was born. He attended Marquette University, was graduated from the University of California at Santa Cruz, and received his Ph.D. from the State University of New York at Buffalo.

His many novels include *Dragonwings*, a Newbery Honor Book of 1976 and the recipient of the International Reading Association's 1976 Children's Book Award, and *Dragon's Gate*, a Newbery Honor Book of 1994. The author of many other books for children and young adults, he has also taught creative writing and Asian American studies at the University of California, Berkeley and Santa Barbara. In 1990 he received an NEA fellowship in fiction.